D0053365

Praise for Lisa McMann's
WAKE

"A lyrical, shuddersome novel whose images linger with you long after you've turned the last page, like the most haunting of dreams."
—Cassandra Clare,
New York Times bestselling author of *City of Ashes*

"A fast-paced, great mix of teen angst and supernatural experiences, and an eerie, attention-grabbing cover will make this a hit."
—*Booklist*

"Every now and then a novel gets published and becomes a work of art that we all will long remember. *Wake* is one of those novels that is not only unique but also mesmerizing and exhilarating. With her debut novel, Lisa McMann creates something that will be on our minds and change the way we think about what we read."
—TeensReadToo.com

"The plot twists keep coming . . . and the writing has a Caroline Cooney–like snap that's hard to resist."
—*Publishers Weekly*

"McMann lures teens in by piquing their interest in the mysteries of the unknown, and keeps them with quick-paced, gripping narration and supportive characters."
—*Kirkus Reviews*

"An economy of language, swift character development, and mysterious circumstances drive the narrative to a fast and . . . satisfying conclusion. McMann also gives useful attention to the science of dreaming."
—*School Library Journal*

An ALA Top Ten Quick Pick
An IRA Young Adult Choice
A Borders Original Voices Nominee
An Association of Booksellers for Children New Voices Selection

ALSO BY
LISA MCMANN

Wake

Fade

Gone

Cryer's Cross

Dead to You

Crash (Visions Book 1)

FOR YOUNGER READERS

The Unwanteds series

The Unwanteds

Island of Silence

The first book in the Wake trilogy

BY LISA MCMANN

SIMON PULSE
NEW YORK LONDON TORONTO SYDNEY NEW DELHI

This one is for you,
Toots

This book is a work of fiction. Any references to historical events, real people, or real places are used fictitiously. Other names, characters, places, and events are products of the author's imagination, and any resemblance to actual events or places or persons, living or dead, is entirely coincidental.

SIMON PULSE
An imprint of Simon & Schuster Children's Publishing Division
1230 Avenue of the Americas, New York, NY 10020

Designed by Mike Rosamilia
The text of this book was set in Janson Text.
Manufactured in the United States of America
First Simon Pulse edition March 2008
10
Library of Congress Cataloging-in-Publication Data
McMann, Lisa.
Wake / Lisa McMann. — 1st Simon Pulse ed.
p. cm.
Summary: Ever since she was eight years old, high school student Janie Hannagan has been uncontrollably drawn into other people's dreams, but it is not until she befriends an elderly nursing home patient and becomes involved with an enigmatic fellow student that she discovers her true power.
ISBN 978-1-4169-5357-9 (hc.)
[Dreams—Fiction. 2. Lucid dreams—Fiction. 3. Emotional problems—Fiction. 4. Undercover operations—Fiction. 5. Interpersonal relations—Fiction. 6. High schools—Fiction. 7. Schools—Fiction.] I. Title.
Pz7.M2256Wak 2008
[Fic]—dc22
2007036267
ISBN 978-1-4169-7447-5 (pbk)
ISBN 978-1-4165-9515-1 (eBook)

ACKNOWLEDGMENTS

To my amazing in-home cheerleaders, house cleaners, and editors—Matt, Kilian, and Kennedy—you rock. There would be no Janie without your love, help, patience, and support.

Special thanks to Dr. Diane Blake Harper, my dear friend and Google-monkey; to Dr. Louis Catron for your kind, priceless critiques; to Ramon Collins for your years of support; and to Tricia, Chris, Erica, Greg, Dawn, Joe, David, Jen, Lisa, Andy, Matthew, Linda, Andie, and Ally for your generous assistance.

Finally, warmest gratitude to my fantastic agent, Michael Bourret, who believed in Janie and in me, and great praises for a most terrific team at Simon Pulse—Jennifer Klonsky, Caroline Abbey, Michael del Rosario, and all the others who help make dreams come true.

SIX MINUTES

December 9, 2005, 12:55 p.m.

Janie Hannagan's math book slips from her fingers. She grips the edge of the table in the school library. Everything goes black and silent. She sighs and rests her head on the table. Tries to pull herself out of it, but fails miserably. She's too tired today. Too hungry. She really doesn't have time for this.

And then.

She's sitting in the bleachers in the football stadium, blinking under the lights, silent among the roars of the crowd.

She glances at the people sitting in the bleachers around her—fellow classmates, parents—trying to spot the dreamer. She can tell this dreamer is afraid, but where is he? Then she looks to the football field. Finds him. Rolls her eyes.

It's Luke Drake. No question about it. He is, after all, the only naked player on the field for the homecoming game.

Nobody seems to notice or care. Except him. The ball is snapped and the lines collide, but Luke is covering himself with his hands, hopping from one foot to the other. She can feel his panic increasing. Janie's fingers tingle and go numb.

Luke looks over at Janie, eyes pleading, as the football moves toward him, a bullet in slow motion. "Help," he says.

She thinks about helping him. Wonders what it would take to change the course of Luke's dream. She even considers that a boost of confidence to the star receiver the day before the big game could put Fieldridge High in the running for the Regional Class A Championship.

But Luke's really a jerk. He won't appreciate it. So she resigns herself to watching the debacle. She wonders if he'll choose pride or glory.

He's not as big as he thinks he is.

That's for damn sure.

The football nearly reaches Luke when the dream starts over again. *Oh, get ON with it already,* Janie thinks. She concentrates in her seat on the bleachers and slowly manages to stand. She tries to walk back under the bleachers for the rest of the dream so she doesn't have to watch, and surprisingly, this time, she is able.

That's a bonus.

1:01 p.m.

Janie's mind catapults back inside her body, still sitting at her usual remote corner table in the library. She flexes her fingers painfully, lifts her head and, when her sight returns, she scours the library.

She spies the culprit at a table about fifteen feet away. He's awake now. Rubbing his eyes and grinning sheepishly at the two other football players who stand around him, laughing. Shoving him. Whapping him on the head.

Janie shakes her head to clear it and she lifts up her math book, which sits open and facedown on the table where she dropped it. Under it, she finds a fun-size Snickers bar. She smiles to herself and peers to the left, between rows of bookshelves.

But no one is there for her to thank.

WHERE IT BEGINS

Evening, December 23, 1996

Janie Hannagan is eight. She wears a thin, faded red-print dress with too-short sleeves, off-white tights that sag between her thighs, gray moon boots, and a brown, nappy coat with two missing buttons. Her long, dirty-blond hair stands up with static. She rides on an Amtrak train with her mother from their home in Fieldridge, Michigan, to Chicago to visit her grandmother. Mother reads the *Globe* across from her. There is a picture on the cover of an enormous man wearing a powder-blue tuxedo. Janie rests her head against the window, watching her breath make a cloud on it.

The cloud blurs Janie's vision so slowly that she doesn't realize what is happening. She floats in the fog for a moment, and then she is in a large room, sitting at a conference table with five men and three women. At the front of the room is a tall, balding man with a briefcase. He stands in his underwear, giving a presentation, and he is flustered. He tries to speak but he can't get his mouth around the words. The other adults are all wearing crisp suits. They laugh and point at the bald man in his underwear.

The bald man looks at Janie.

And then he looks at the people who are laughing at him.

His face crumples in defeat.

He holds his briefcase in front of his privates, and that makes the others laugh harder. He runs to the door of the conference room, but the handle is slippery—something slimy drips from it. He can't get it open; it squeaks and rattles loudly in his hand, and the people at the table double over. The man's underwear is grayish-white, sagging. He turns to Janie again, with a look of panic and pleading.

Janie doesn't know what to do.

She freezes.

The train's brakes whine.

And the scene grows cloudy and is lost in fog.

"Janie!" Janie's mother is leaning toward Janie. Her breath smells like gin, and her straggly hair falls over one eye. "Janie, I said, maybe Grandma will take you to that big fancy doll store. I thought you would be excited about that, but I guess not." Janie's mother sips from a flask in her ratty old purse.

Janie focuses on her mother and smiles. "That sounds fun," she says, even though she doesn't like dolls. She would rather have new tights. She wriggles on the seat, trying to adjust them. The crotch stretches tight at mid-thigh. She thinks about the bald man and scrunches her eyes. *Weird.*

When the train stops, they take their bags and step into the aisle. In front of Janie's mother, a disheveled, bald businessman emerges from his compartment.

He wipes his face with a handkerchief.

Janie stares at him.

Her jaw drops. "Whoa," she whispers.

The man gives her a bland look when he sees her staring, and turns to exit the train.

September 6, 1999, 3:05 p.m.

Janie sprints to catch the bus after her first day of sixth grade. Melinda Jeffers, one of the Fieldridge North Side girls, sticks her foot out, sending Janie sprawling across the gravel. Melinda laughs all the way to her mother's shiny red Jeep Cherokee. Janie fights back the urge to cry, and dusts herself off. She climbs on the bus, flops into the front seat, and looks at the dirt and blood on the palms of her hands, and the rip in the knee of her already well-worn pants.

Sixth grade makes her throat hurt.

She leans her head against the window.

When she gets home, Janie walks past her mother, who is on the couch watching *Guiding Light* and drinking from a clear glass bottle. Janie washes her stinging hands carefully, dries them, and sits down next to her mother, hoping she'll notice. Hoping she'll say something.

But Janie's mother is asleep now.

Her mouth is open.

She snores lightly.

The bottle tips in her hand.

Janie sighs, sets the bottle on the beat-up coffee table, and starts her homework.

Halfway through her math homework, the room turns black.

Janie is rushed into a bright tunnel, like a multicolored

kaleidoscope. There's no floor, and Janie is floating while the walls spin around her. It makes her feel like throwing up.

Next to Janie in the tunnel is her mother, and a man who looks like a blond Jesus Christ. The man and Janie's mother are holding hands and flying. They look happy. Janie yells, but no sound comes out. She wants it to stop.

She feels the pencil fall from her fingers.

Feels her body slump to the arm of the couch.

Tries to sit up, but with all the whirling colors around her, she can't tell which way is upright. She overcompensates and falls the other way, onto her mother.

The colors stop, and everything goes black.

Janie hears her mother grumbling.

Feels her shove.

Slowly the room comes into focus again, and Janie's mother slaps Janie in the face.

"Get offa me," her mother says. "What the hell is wrong with you?"

Janie sits up and looks at her mother. Her stomach churns, and she feels dizzy from the colors. "I feel sick," she whispers, and then she stands up and stumbles to the bathroom to vomit.

When she peers out, pale and shaky, her mother is gone from the couch, retired to her bedroom.

Thank God, Janie thinks. She splashes cold water on her face.

January 1, 2001, 7:29 a.m.

A U-Haul truck pulls up next door. A man, a woman, and a girl Janie's age climb out and sink into the snow-covered driveway. Janie watches them from her bedroom window.

The girl is dark-haired and pretty.

Janie wonders if she'll be snooty, like all the other girls who call Janie white trash at school. Maybe, since this new girl lives next to Janie on the wrong side of town, they'll call her white trash too.

But she's really pretty.

Pretty enough to make a difference.

Janie dresses hurriedly, puts on her boots and coat, and marches next door to have the first chance to get to the girl before the North Siders get to her. Janie's desperate for a friend.

"You guys want some help?" Janie asks in a voice more confident than she feels.

The girl stops in her tracks. A smile deepens the dimples in her cheeks, and she tilts her head to the side. "Hi," she says. "I'm Carrie Brandt."

Carrie's eyes sparkle.

Janie's heart leaps.

March 2, 2001, 7:34 p.m.

Janie is thirteen.

She doesn't have a sleeping bag, but Carrie has an extra that Janie can use. Janie sets her plastic grocery bag on the floor by the couch in Carrie's living room.

Inside the bag:
a hand-made birthday gift for Carrie
Janie's pajamas
a toothbrush

She's nervous. But Carrie is chattering enough for both of them, waiting for Carrie's other new friend, Melinda Jeffers, to show up.

Yes, that Melinda Jeffers.

Of the Fieldridge North Side Jefferses.

Apparently, Melinda Jeffers is also the president of the "Make Janie Hannagan Miserable" Club. Janie wipes her sweating hands on her jeans.

When Melinda arrives, Carrie doesn't fawn over her. Janie nods hello.

Melinda smirks. Tries to whisper something to Carrie, but Carrie ignores her and says, "Hey! Let's do Janie's hair."

Melinda throws a daggered look at Carrie.

Carrie smiles brightly at Janie, asking her with her eyes if it's okay.

Janie squelches a grin, and Melinda shrugs and pretends like she doesn't mind after all.

Even though Janie knows it's killing her.

The three girls slowly grow more comfortable, or maybe just resigned, with one another. They put on make-up and watch Carrie's favorite videos of old comedians, some of whom Janie's never heard of before. And then they play truth or dare.

Carrie alternates: truth, dare, truth, dare.

Melinda always picks truth.

And then there's Janie.

Janie never picks truth.

She's a dare girl.

That way, nobody gets inside.

She can't afford to let anyone inside.

They might find out about her secret.

The giggles become hysterics when Melinda's dare for Janie is to run outside through the snow barefoot, around to the backyard, take off her clothes, and make a naked snow angel.

Janie doesn't have a problem doing that.

Because, really, what does she have to lose?

She'll take that dare over giving up her secrets any day.

Melinda watches Janie, arms folded in the cold night air, and with a sneer on her face, while Carrie giggles and helps Janie get her sweatshirt and jeans back on her wet body. Carrie takes Janie's bra, fills the cups with snow, and slingshots them like snowballs at Melinda.

"Ew, gross," Melinda sneers. "Where'd you get that old grungy thing, Salvation Army?"

Janie's giggles fade. She grabs her bra back from Carrie and shoves it in her jeans pocket, embarrassed. "No," she says hotly, then giggles again. "It was Goodwill. Why, does it look familiar?"

Carrie snorts.

Even Melinda laughs, reluctantly.

They trudge back inside for popcorn.

11:34 p.m.

The noise level in the living room of Carrie's house fades along with the lights after Mr. Brandt, Carrie's father, stomps to the doorway and hollers at the three girls to shut up and get to sleep.

Janie zips up the musty-smelling sleeping bag and closes her eyes, but she is too hyper to sleep after that exhilarating naked snow angel. She had a fun evening despite Melinda. She learned what it's like to be a rich girl (sounds nice for about a day, but too many stinking lessons), and that Luke Drake is supposedly the hottest boy in the class (in Carrie's mind), and what people like Melinda do four times a year (they take vacations to exotic places). Who knew?

Now the hushed giggles subside around her, and Janie opens her eyes to stare at the dark ceiling. She is glad to be here, even though Melinda teases her about her clothes. Melinda even had the nerve to ask Janie why she never wears anything new. But Carrie shut her up with a sudden exclamation: "Janie, you look simply stunning with your hair back like that. Doesn't she, Melinda?"

For the first time ever, Janie's hair is in French braids, and now, lying in the sleeping bag, she feels the bumps pressing against her scalp through the thin pillow. Maybe Carrie could teach her how to do it sometime.

She has to pee, but she is afraid to get up, in case Carrie's father hears her and starts yelling again. She rests quietly like the other girls, listening to them breathe as they drift off to sleep. Melinda is in the middle, curled on her side facing Carrie, her back to Janie.

12:14 a.m.

The ceiling clouds over and disappears. Janie blinks and she is at school, in civics class. She looks around and realizes she is not in her normal fourth-period class, but in the class that follows hers. She stands at the back of the room. There are no empty seats. Ms. Parchelli, the teacher, drones about the judicial branch of government and what the Supreme Court justices wear under their robes. No one seems surprised that Ms. Parchelli is teaching them this. Some of the kids take notes.

Janie looks around at the faces in the room. In the third row, seated at the center desk, is Melinda. Melinda has a dreamy look on her face. She is staring at someone in the next row, one seat forward. As the teacher talks, Melinda stands up slowly and approaches the person she's been staring at. From the back of the room, Janie cannot see who it is.

The teacher doesn't appear to notice. Melinda kneels next to the desk and touches the person's hand. In slow motion, the person turns to Melinda, touches her cheek, and then leans forward. The two of them kiss. After a moment, they both rise to their feet, still kissing. When they part, Janie can see the face of Melinda's kissing partner. Melinda leads her partner by the hand to the front of the room and opens the door of the supply closet. The bell rings, and like ants, the students crowd at the door to leave.

The ceiling in Carrie Brandt's living room reappears as Melinda sighs and flops onto her stomach in the sleeping bag next to Janie. *Cripes!* thinks Janie. She looks at the clock. It's 1:23 a.m.

1:24 a.m.

Janie rolls to her side and she's walking into a forest. It's dark from shade, not night. A few rays of weak sunlight slip through the tree cover. Walking in front of Janie is Carrie. They walk for what seems to be a mile or more, and suddenly a rushing river appears a few steps in front of them. Carrie stops and cups her ear, listening for something. She calls out in a desperate voice, "Carson!" Over and over, Carrie calls the name, until the forest rings with her voice. Carrie walks along the high bank and stumbles over a tree root. Janie bumps into her, falls, and then Carrie helps her up. She gives Janie a puzzled look and says, "You've never been here." Carrie turns back to her search for Carson, her cries growing louder.

There is a splash in the river, and a little boy appears above the surface, bobbing and moving swiftly in the current. Carrie runs along the bank and cries, "Carson! Get out of there! Carson!"

The boy grins and chokes on the water. He goes under and resurfaces. Carrie is frantic. She reaches out her hand to the boy, but it makes no difference—the bank is too high, the river too wide for her to come close to reaching him. She is crying now.

Janie watches, her heart pounding. The boy is still grinning and choking, falling under the water. He is drowning.

"Help him!" screams Carrie. "Save him!"

Janie leaps toward the boy in the water, but she lands on

the bank in the same spot she took off from. She tries again as Carrie screams, but the results are the same.

The boy's eyes are closed now. His grin has turned eerie. From the water behind the boy, an enormous shark bursts above the surface, mouth open, hundreds of sharp teeth gleaming. It closes its mouth around the boy and disappears.

Carrie sits up in her sleeping bag and screams.

Janie screams too, but it catches in her throat.

Her voice is hoarse.

Her fingers are numb.

Her body shakes from the nightmare.

The two girls look at each other in the darkness, while Melinda stirs, groans, and goes back to sleep. "Are you okay?" Janie whispers, sitting up.

Carrie nods, breathing hard. She whisper-laughs, embarrassed. Her voice shakes. "I'm sorry I woke you. Bad dream."

Janie hesitates. "You want to talk about it?" Her mind is racing.

"Nah. Go back to sleep." Carrie rolls to her side. Melinda stirs, rolls a few inches closer to Carrie, and is quiet again.

Janie glances at the clock. 3:42 a.m. She is exhausted. She drifts off to sleep. . . .

3:51 a.m.

. . . she is jolted awake when she falls into a huge, beautiful bedroom. There are framed posters of *NSYNC and Sheryl Crow on the walls. At a desk sits Melinda, doodling on the edge of her notebook. Janie tries to blink herself out of the room. She feels herself sit up in the sleeping bag, but her motions don't affect what she sees. She lies back down, resigned to watch.

Melinda is drawing hearts. Janie walks toward her. She says, "Melinda," but no sound comes out. When someone knocks on the bedroom window, Melinda looks over and smiles. "Help me open this window, will you?"

Janie stares at Melinda. Melinda stares back, then points to the window with a jerk of her head. Janie, feeling compelled, stumbles over to the window next to Melinda and they open it. Carrie climbs in.

She is naked from the waist up.

And has breasts the size of watermelons.

The breasts sway from side to side when Carrie scrambles over the sill.

She walks through Janie and stands shyly in front of Melinda.

Janie tries to turn away, but she can't. She waves a hand in front of Carrie's face, but Carrie doesn't respond. Melinda winks at Janie and folds Carrie into her arms. They embrace and kiss. Janie rolls her eyes, and suddenly all three are back in Ms. Parchelli's civics classroom. Once again, Melinda is embracing someone in the aisle. It's Carrie. She leads Carrie to the front of the room. Janie can see that no one else in the class gives an ounce of notice to the naked Carrie and her enormous breasts.

Janie sits up in her sleeping bag again and shakes her head wildly. She feels the ends of her braids slap the sides of her cheeks, but she is unable to remove herself from the classroom. She is forced not only to be there, but also to watch.

Melinda glides to the supply closet and leads Carrie in there with her. Janie, against her wishes, follows. Melinda closes the door once Carrie and Janie are inside, and Melinda starts kissing Carrie on the lips again.

Janie lunges in her sleeping bag blindly.

Kicks Melinda, hard.

And Janie is back in Carrie's living room.

Melinda sits up, hair disheveled, and scrambles around to look at Janie. "What the hell did you do that for?" Melinda is furious.

Feigning sleep, Janie peers out of one eye. "Sorry," she mumbles. "There was a spider crawling over your sleeping bag. I saved your life."

"What?!"

"Never mind, he's gone."

"Oh, great. Like I'm gonna get back to sleep now."

Janie grins in the darkness. It's 5:51 a.m.

7:45 a.m.

Something nudges Janie's legs. She opens her eyes, wondering where she is. It's pitch dark. Carrie turns the sleeping bag flap off Janie's head. "Wake up, sleepyhead." The sunlight is blinding.

"Mmph," Janie grunts. Slowly she sits up.

Carrie is balancing on her haunches, eyeing her, one brow raised.

Janie remembers. Does Carrie?

"Did you sleep well?" Carrie asks.

Janie's stomach twists. "Um . . . yeah." She gauges Carrie's reaction. "Did you?"

Carrie smiles. "Like a baby. Even on this hard floor."

"Ah, hmm. Well, that's great." Janie scrambles to her feet and untwists from her nightgown. "Where's Melinda?"

"She left about ten minutes ago. She was acting weird. Said she forgot she had a piano lesson at eight." Carrie snorts. "Duh."

Janie laughs weakly. She's starving. The two girls fix breakfast. Carrie doesn't appear to remember her nightmare.

Janie can't forget it.

As they munch on toast, Janie steals a glance at Carrie's chest. Her breasts are the size of half an apple, each.

Janie goes home, falls into bed, thinking about the strange night. Wondering if this ever happens to anyone else. Knowing, deep down, it probably doesn't.

She falls into a hard sleep until late afternoon.

Decides sleepovers are not for her.

They'll never be for her.

June 7, 2004

Janie is sixteen. She buys her own clothing now. Often she buys food, too. The welfare check covers the rent and the booze, and not much else.

Two years ago, Janie started working a few hours after school and on the weekends at Heather Nursing Home. Now she works full-time for the summer.

The office staff and the other aides at Heather Home like Janie, especially during school holidays, because she'll pick up anybody's shifts, day or night, so they can take a last-minute sick day or vacation. Janie needs the money, and they know it.

She's determined to go to college.

Five days a week or more, Janie puts on her hospital scrubs and takes a bus to the nursing home. She likes old people. They don't sleep soundly.

Janie and Carrie are still friends and next-door neighbors. They spend a lot of time at Janie's house, waiting for Janie's mother to pass out in her bedroom before they watch movies and talk about boys. They talk about other things too, like why Carrie's father is so angry all the time, and why Carrie's mother doesn't like company. Mostly, Janie thinks, it's just because they're grouchy people. Plain and simple. Whenever Carrie asks if she can have Janie sleep over, her mother says, "You just had a sleepover on your birthday." Carrie doesn't bother to remind her that that was four years ago.

Janie thinks about Carson and wonders if Carrie really is an only child. But Carrie doesn't seem to talk about anything with sharp edges. Maybe she's afraid they might poke into her and then she'd burst.

Carrie and Melinda are also still friends. Melinda's parents are still rich. Melinda plays tennis. She is a cheerleader. Her parents have condos in Vegas, Marco Island, Vail, and somewhere in Greece. Melinda mostly hangs out with other rich kids. And then there's Carrie.

Janie doesn't mind being with Melinda. Melinda still can't stand Janie. Janie thinks she knows the real reason why, and it doesn't have anything to do with having money.

June 25, 2004, 11:15 p.m.

After working a record eleven evenings straight, and being caught by old Mr. Reed's recurring nightmare about World War II seven of those eleven evenings, Janie collapses on the couch and kicks her shoes off. By the number of empty bottles on the ring-stained coffee table, she assumes her mother is in her bedroom, down for the count.

Carrie lets herself in. "Can I crash here?" Her eyes are rimmed in red.

Janie sighs inwardly. She wants to sleep. "'Course. You okay with the couch?"

"Sure. Thanks."

Janie relaxes. Carrie, on the couch, would work fine.

Carrie sniffles loudly.

"So, what's wrong?" Janie asks, trying to put as much sympathy in her voice as she can muster. It's enough.

"Dad's yelling again. I got asked out. Dad says no."

Janie perks up. "Who asked you out?"

"Stu. From the body shop."

"You mean that old guy?"

Carrie bristles. "He's twenty-two."

"You're sixteen! And he looks older than that."

"Not up close. He's cute. He has a cute ass."

"Maybe he plays Dance Dance Revolution at the arcade."

Carrie giggles. Janie smiles.

"So. You got any liquor around here?" Carrie asks innocently.

Janie laughs. "There's an understatement. Whaddya want, beer?" She looks at the bottles on the table. "Schnapps? Whiskey? Double-stuff vodka?"

"Got any of that cheap grape wine the winos at Selby Park drink?"

"At your service." Janie hauls herself off the couch and looks for clean glasses. The kitchen is a mess. Janie has barely been here the past two weeks. She finds two sticky, mismatched glasses in the sink and washes them out, then searches through her mother's stash for her cheap wine assortment. "Ah, here it is. Boone's Farm, right?" She unscrews the bottle and pours two glasses full, not waiting for an answer from Carrie, and then puts the bottle back in the fridge.

Carrie flips on the TV. She takes a glass from Janie. "Thanks."

Janie sips the sweet wine and makes a face. "So what are you gonna do about Stu?" She thinks there's a country song in that sentence somewhere.

"Go out with him."

"Your dad's gonna kill you if he finds out."

"Yeah, well. What else is new?" They both settle on the creaky couch and put their feet on the coffee table, deftly pushing the mess of bottles to the center of it so they can stretch out.

The TV drones. The girls sip their wine and get silly. Janie gets up, rummages around in her bedroom, and returns with snacks.

"Gross—you keep Doritos in your bedroom?"

"Emergency stash. For nights such as these." *Since Mother can't be bothered to buy any actual food at the grocery store when she goes there for booze*, Janie thinks.

"Ahh." Carrie nods.

12:30 a.m.

Janie is asleep on the couch. She doesn't dream. Never dreams.

5:02 a.m.

Janie, forced awake, catapults into Carrie's dream. It's the one by the river. Again. Janie's been here twice since the first time, when they were thirteen.

Janie, blind to the room her physical body is in, tries to stand. If she can feel her way to her bedroom and close the door before she starts going numb, she might get enough distance to break the connection. She feels with her toes for the bottles on the floor, and goes around them. She reaches out for the wall and finds her way into the hallway as she and Carrie are walking through the forest in Carrie's dream. Janie reaches for the door frames—first her mother's bedroom (hush, don't bump the door), then the bathroom, and then her room. She makes it inside, turns, and closes the door just as Carrie and Janie approach the riverbank.

The connection is lost.

Janie breathes a sigh of relief. She looks around, blinks in the dark as her eyesight returns, crawls into bed, and sleeps.

9:06 a.m.

When she wakes, both her mother and Carrie are in the kitchen. The living room is cleared of bottles. Carrie is drying a sink full of dishes, and Janie's mother is fixing her homemade morning drink: vodka and orange juice on ice. On the stove is a skillet covered by a paper plate. Two pieces of buttered toast, two eggs over easy, and a small fortune of crisp bacon rest on a second paper plate, next to the skillet. Janie's mother picks up a piece of bacon, takes her drink, and disappears back into her bedroom without a word.

"Thanks Carrie—you didn't have to do this. I was planning on cleaning today."

Carrie is cheerful. "It's the least I can do. Did you sleep well? When did you go to bed?"

Janie peeks in the skillet, thinking, discovering hash

browns. "Wow! Um . . . not long ago. It was close to daylight. But I was so tired."

"You've been working ridiculous hours."

Janie. "Yeah, well. College. One day. How did you sleep?"

"Pretty good . . ." She hesitates, like she might say something else, but doesn't.

Janie takes a bite of food. She's famished. "Did you have sweet dreams?"

Carrie glances at Janie, then picks up another dish and wipes it with the towel. "Not really."

Janie concentrates on the food, but her stomach flips. She waits, until the silence grows awkward. "You want to talk about it?"

Carrie is silent for a long time. "Not really. No," she says finally.

AND PICKS UP SPEED

August 30, 2004

It is the first day of school. Janie and Carrie are juniors. They wait for the bus on the corner of their street. A handful of other high school kids stand with them. Some are anxious. Some are terribly short. Janie and Carrie ignore the freshmen.

The bus is late. Luckily for Cabel Strumheller, the bus is later than he is. Janie and Carrie know Cabel—he's been trouble in school since ninth grade. Janie doesn't remember him much before that—word was that he flunked down into their grade. He was often late. Always looked stoned. Now, he looks about six inches taller than he did in the spring. His blue-black hair hangs in greasy ringlets in front of his eyes, and he walks with shoulders curved, as if he were more comfortable being short. He stands away from everyone and smokes a cigarette.

Janie catches his eye by accident, so she nods hello. He looks down at the ground quickly. Blows smoke from his lips. Tosses the cigarette down and grinds it into the gravel.

Carrie pokes Janie in the ribs. "Lookie, it's your boyfriend."

Janie rolls her eyes. "Be nice."

Carrie observes him carefully while he's not looking. "Well. His pox-face cleared up over the summer. Or maybe the new fancy 'do hides it."

"Stop," hisses Janie. She's giggling, and feeling bad about it. But she's looking at him. He's got to be about as dirt poor as Janie, judging by his clothes. "He's just a loner. And quiet."

"A stoner, maybe, who has a boner for you."

Janie narrows her eyes, and her face grows sober. "Carrie, stop it. I'm serious. You're turning mean like Melinda." Janie glances at Cabel. His jeans are too short. She knows what it's like to be teased for not having cool clothes and stuff. She feels herself wanting to defend him. "He probably has shitty welfare parents, like me."

Carrie is quiet. "I'm not like Melinda."

"So why do you hang with her?"

She shrugs and thinks about it for a minute. "I dunno. 'Cause she's rich."

Finally the bus comes. The ride is forty-five minutes to school, even though the school is less than five miles away, because of all the stops. Juniors like Janie and Carrie are considered by the unwritten bus rules to be upperclassmen. So they sit near the back. Cabel passes by and falls into the seat behind them. Janie can feel him push his knees up against her back. She peers through the crack between her seat back and the window. Cabel's chin is propped up by his hand. His eyes are closed, nearly hidden beneath his greasy curls.

"Fuck," Janie mutters under her breath.

Thankfully, Cabel Strumheller doesn't dream.

Not on the bus, anyway.

Not in chemistry class, either.

Or English.

Nor does anyone else. Janie arrives home after the first day of school, relieved.

October 16, 2004, 7:42 p.m.

Carrie and Stu knock on Janie's bedroom window. She opens it a crack. Stu's dressed up, wearing a thin, black leather tie, and Carrie has on a slinky black dress with a shawl and a hideously large orchid pinned to it.

"I saw your light on in here," explains Carrie, regarding the unusual visit. "Come to the homecoming dance, with us, Janers! We're not staying long. Please?"

Janie sighs. "You know I don't have anything to wear."

Carrie holds up a silver spaghetti-strap dress so Janie can see it. "Here—I bet this'll fit you. I got it from Melinda. She'll die if she sees you in it instead of me. And I've got shoes that'll go with it." Carrie grins evilly.

"I haven't washed my hair or anything."

"You look fine, Janie," Stu says. "Come on. Don't make me sit there with a bunch of teenybopper airheads all night. Have pity on an old man."

Janie smirks. Carrie slaps Stu on the arm.

She meets them at the front door, takes the dress, and heads over to Carrie's ten minutes later.

9:12 p.m.

Janie drinks her third cup of punch while Stu and Carrie dance for the billionth time. She sits down at a table, alone.

9:18 p.m.

A sophomore boy, known only to Janie as "the brainiac," asks Janie to dance.

She regards him for a moment. "Why the fuck not," she says. She's a head taller than him.

He rests his head on her chest and grabs her ass.

She pushes him off her, muttering under her breath, finds Carrie, and tells her she has a ride home and she's leaving now.

Carrie waves blissfully from Stu's arms.

Janie attacks the back door of the school gym and finds herself in a heavy cloud of smoke. She realizes she's found the Goths' hangout. Who knew?

"Oof," someone says. She keeps walking, muttering "sorry" to whomever it was she hit with the flying door.

After a mile wearing Carrie's heels, her feet are killing her. She takes off the shoes and walks in the grassy yards, watching the houses evolve from nice to nasty as she goes along. The grass is already wet with dew, and the yards are getting messier. Her feet are freezing.

Someone falls in step beside her, so quietly that she doesn't notice him until he's there. He's carrying a skateboard. A second and third follow suit, then lay their boards down and push off, hanging slightly in front of Janie.

"Jeez!" she says, surrounded. "Scare a girl half to death, why don't you."

Cabel Strumheller shrugs. The other guys move ahead. "Long walk," says Cabel. "You, uh"—he clears his throat—"okay?"

"Fine," she says. "You?" She doesn't remember ever hearing him speak before.

"Get on." He sets his board down, taking Janie's shoes from her hand. "You'll rip your feet to shreds. There's glass an' shit."

Janie looks at the board, and then up at him. He's wearing a knit beanie with a hole in it. "I don't know how."

He flashes a half grin. Shoves a long black lock of hair under the beanie. "Just stand. Bend. Balance. I'll push you."

She blinks. Gets on the board.

Weird.

This is not happening.

They don't talk.

The guys weave in and out the rest of the way, and take off at the corner by Janie's house. Cabel pushes her to her front porch so she can hop off. He sets her shoes on the step, picks up the board, nods, and catches up with his friends.

"Thanks, Cabel," Janie says, but he's gone in the dark already. "That was sweet," she adds, to no one.

They don't acknowledge each other, or the event, for a very long time.

IN EARNEST

February 1, 2005

Janie is seventeen.

A boy named Jack Tomlinson falls asleep in English class. Janie watches his head nodding from across the room. She begins to sweat, even though the room is cold. It is 11:41 a.m. Seven minutes until the bell rings for lunch. Too much time.

She stands, gathers her books, and rushes for the door. “I feel sick,” she says to the teacher. The teacher nods understandingly. Melinda Jeffers snickers from the back row. Janie leaves the room and shuts the door.

She leans against the cool tile wall, takes a deep breath, goes into the girls' bathroom, and hides in a stall.

Nobody ever sleeps in the bathroom.

Flashback—January 9, 1998

It's Janie's tenth birthday. Tanya Weersma falls asleep in school, her head on her pencil box. She is floating, gliding. And then she is falling. Falling into a gorge. The face of a cliff streams by at a dizzying speed. Tanya looks at Janie and screams. Janie closes her eyes and feels sick. They startle at the same time. The fourth graders all laugh.

Janie decides not to hand out her precious birthday treat, after all.

That was after the train ride and the man in the underwear.

Janie's had only a few close calls in school before high school. But the older she gets, the more often her classmates sleep in school. And the more kids sleep, the more of a mess it makes for Janie. She has to get away, wake them up, or risk the consequences.

A year and a half to go.

And then.

College. A roommate.

Janie puts her head in her hands.

She leaves the bathroom after lunch and goes to her next class, grabbing a Snickers bar on her way.

For two weeks afterward, Melinda Jeffers and her rich friends make puking noises when they pass Janie in the hall.

June 15, 2005

Janie is seventeen. She's working her ass off, taking as many shifts as she can.

Old Mr. Reed is dying at the nursing home.

His dreams grow constant and terrible.

He doesn't wake easily.

As his body fades, the pull of his dreams grows eerily stronger. Now, if his door is open, Janie can't enter that wing.

She hadn't planned for this.

She makes an odd request on every shift. "If you cover the east wing, I'll take the rest."

The other aides think she's afraid to see Mr. Reed die.

Janie doesn't have a problem with that.

June 21, 2005, 9:39 p.m.

Heather Home is short-staffed. It's summer. Three patients on the cusp of death. Two have Alzheimer's. One dreams, screams, and cries.

Someone has to empty bedpans. Hand out the night meds. Straighten up the rooms for the day.

Janie approaches with caution. She stands in the west wing, looking into the east wing, and memorizes it. The right-hand wall has five doorways and six sets of handrails. The last door on the right is Mr. Reed. Ten steps farther is a wall, and the emergency exit door.

Some days, a cart stands between doorways three and four. Some days, wheelchairs collect anonymously between doorways one and two. A stretcher often rests in the east wing, but usually it's on the left side. Janie would have to get a glimpse before entering the hallway, no matter the day. Because some days, most days, people travel up and down the hallway without pattern. And Janie doesn't want to run into anyone in case she goes blind.

Tonight, the hallway is clear. Janie noted earlier that the Silva family came for a visit in the fourth room. She checks the record book and sees that they signed out. There are no other visitors recorded. It grows late. For Janie, it's either get the work done, or get fired.

She enters the east wing, grabs the hall bar, and nearly doubles over.

9:41 p.m.

The noise of the battle is overpowering. She hides with old Mr. Reed in a foxhole on a beach that is littered with bodies and watered with blood. The scene is so familiar, Janie could recite the conversation—even the beat of the bullets—by heart. And it always ends the same way, with arms and legs scattered, bones crunching underfoot, and Mr. Reed's body breaking into tiny bits, crumbling off his trunk like cheese being grated from a slab, or like a leper, unraveling.

Janie tries walking normally down the hallway, gripping the handrail. She cannot concentrate enough to remember her count of doorways, the dream is so intense. She keeps walking, reaching, walking, until she hits the wall. She's losing the feeling in her fingers and feet. Wants to make it stop. She backs up eight, ten, maybe twelve steps, and falls to the ground outside Mr. Reed's door. Her head pounds now as she follows Mr. Reed into battle.

She tries to find his door so she can close it. She tries, and she can't feel anything. She doesn't know if she's touching something, or nothing. She is paralyzed. Numb. Desperate.

On the bloody beach, Mr. Reed looks at her and beckons her to come with him. "Behind here. We'll be safe behind here," he says.

"No!" she tries to scream, but no sound comes out. She can't get his attention. *Not behind there!* She knows what will happen.

Mr. Reed's fingers drop off first.

Then his nose and ears.

He looks at Janie.

Like always.

Like she's betrayed him.

"Why didn't you tell me," he whispers.

Janie can't speak, can't move. Again and again, she fights, her head feeling like it might explode any moment. *Just die, old man!* she wants to yell. *I can't do this one anymore!* She knows it's almost over.

And then, there is more. Something new.

Mr. Reed turns to her as his feet break free from his ankles and he stumbles on his stilty legs. His eyes are wide with terror, and the battle rages around them. "Come closer," he says. Fingerless, he shrugs the gun into her arms. His arm breaks off his shoulder as he does it, and it crumbles to the beach like powder. And then he starts crying. "Help me. Help me, Janie."

Janie's eyes widen. She sees the enemy, but she knows they can't see her. She is safe. She looks at the pleading eyes of Mr. Reed.

Lifts the gun.

Points.

And pulls the trigger.

10:59 p.m.

Janie is curled on a portable stretcher in the east hallway when the roaring gunfire in old Mr. Reed's dream stops abruptly. She blinks, her vision clears slowly, and she sees two Heather Home aides staring down at her. She sits up halfway. Her head pounds.

"Careful, Janie, honey," soothes a voice. "You were having a seizure or something. Let's wait for the doc, okay?"

Janie cocks her head and listens for the faint sound of beeping. A moment later, she hears it.

"Old Mr. Reed is dead," she says, her voice rasping. She falls back on the stretcher and passes out.

June 22, 2005

The doctor says, "We need to do some tests. Do a CAT scan."

"No thank you," Janie says. She is polite, but firm.

The doctor looks at Janie's mother. "Mrs. Hannagan?"

Janie's mother shrugs. She looks out the window. Her hands tremble as she fingers the zipper on her purse.

The doctor sighs, exasperated. "Ma'am," he tries again. "What if she has a seizure while she's driving? Or crossing a street? Please think about it."

Mrs. Hannagan closes her eyes.

Janie clears her throat. "May we go?"

The doctor gives Janie a long look. He glances at Janie's mother, who is looking down at her lap. Then looks at Janie again. "Of course," he says softly. "Can you promise me something? Not just for your safety, but for the safety of others on the road—please, don't drive."

It won't happen when I'm driving, she longs to tell him, just so he doesn't worry so much. "Sure. I promise. We don't have a car, anyway."

Mrs. Hannagan stands. Janie stands. The doctor stands too. "Call our office if it happens again, won't you?" He holds out his hand, and Janie shakes it.

"Yes," Janie lies. They walk back to the waiting room.

Janie sends her mother outside to the bus stop. "I'll be right there."

Her mother leaves the office. Janie pays the bill. It's $120, pulled out of her college stash. She can only imagine how much a CAT scan would cost. And she's not about to spend another cent just to hear somebody tell her she's crazy.

She can get that opinion for free.

Janie waits for her mother to ask what that was all about. But she may as well wait for flowers to grow on the moon. Janie's mother simply doesn't care about anything that has to do with Janie. She has never really cared.

And that's fucking sad.

That's what Janie thinks.

But it sure comes in handy, sometimes.

June 28, 2005

There's something about a doctor telling a teenager not to drive that makes it so important to do so. Just to prove him wrong.

Janie and Carrie go see Stu at the body shop. He sees them coming. "Here she is, kiddo," Stu says. He calls Janie "kiddo," which is weird, since Janie is two months older than Carrie.

Janie nods and smiles. She runs her hand over the hood lightly, feeling the curves. It's the color of buttermilk. It's older than Janie. And it's beautiful.

Stu hands Janie the keys, and Janie counts out one thousand, four hundred fifty dollars cash. "Be good to her," he says wistfully. "I started working on this car when she was seventeen years old and I was thirteen. She purrs now."

"I will." Janie smiles. She climbs in the '77 Nova and starts her up.

"Her name's Ethel," adds Stu. He looks a little embarrassed.

Carrie takes Stu's oil-stained hand and squeezes it. "Janie's a really good driver. She's driven my car a bunch of times. Ethel will be fine." She gives Stu a quick kiss on the cheek. "See you tonight," she says with a demure smile.

Stu winks. Carrie gets into her Tracer and Janie slides behind the wheel of her new car. She pats the dashboard, and Ethel purrs. "Good girl, Ethel," she croons.

June 29, 2005

After the incident with Mr. Reed, the Heather Home director made Janie take a week off. When Janie shuffled and hemmed about taking that much time off, the director promised her shifts on July 4 and Labor Day, where Janie gets double pay. She is happy.

Janie drives her new car on her first day back to work. She gives sponge baths and empties a dozen bedpans. For entertainment, she sings a mournful song from *Les Misérables*, changing the words to "Empty pans and empty bladders . . ." Miss Stubin, a schoolteacher who taught for forty-seven years before she retired, laughs for the first time in weeks. Janie makes a mental note to bring in a new book to read to Miss Stubin.

Miss Stubin never has visitors.

And she's blind.

That just might be why she's Janie's favorite.

July 4, 2005, 10:15 p.m.

Three Heather Home residents in their wheelchairs, and Janie, in an orange plastic bucket chair, sit in the dark nursing home parking lot. Waiting. Slapping mosquitoes. The fireworks are about to begin at Selby Park, a few blocks away.

Miss Stubin is one of the residents, her gnarled hands curled in her lap, I.V. drip hanging from a stand next to her wheelchair. All of a sudden, she cocks her head and smiles wistfully. "Here they come," she says.

A moment later, the sky explodes in color.

Janie describes each one in detail to Miss Stubin.

A green sparkly porcupine, she says.

Sparks rising from a magician's wand.

A perfect circle of white light, which fades into a puddle and dries up.

After a brilliant burst of purple, Janie jumps up. "Don't go anywhere, you three—I'll be right back." She runs inside to the therapy room, grabs a plastic tub, and runs back out.

"Here," she says breathlessly, taking Miss Stubin's hand and carefully, gently, stretching out her curled fingers. She puts a Koosh Ball in the old woman's hands. "That last one looked just like this."

Miss Stubin's face lights up. "I think that's my favorite," she says.

August 2, 2005, 11:11 p.m.

Janie leaves Heather Home and drives the four miles to her house. It's wicked hot out, and she chides Ethel mildly for not having air-conditioning. She rolls the windows down, loving the feeling of the hot wind on her face.

11:18 p.m.

She stops at a stop sign on Waverly Road, not far from home, and proceeds through the intersection.

11:19 p.m.

And then she is in a strange house. In a dirty kitchen. A huge, young monster-man with knives for fingers approaches.

Janie, blind to the road, stomps on the brake and flips the gearshift into neutral. She reaches to find the emergency brake and pulls, before she becomes paralyzed. This is a strong one.

He pulls a vinyl-seated chair across the kitchen floor, picks it up, and whirls it around above his head.

But it isn't the emergency brake. It's the hood release.

And then he lets go of the chair. It sails toward Janie, clipping the ceiling fan.

Janie doesn't know it's the hood.

She looks around frantically to see what it will hit. Or who.

Janie is numb. Her foot slides off the brake pedal.
Her car rolls off the road.
Slowly.

But there is no one else. No one else but the monster-man with finger-knives, and Janie. Until the door opens, and a middle-aged man appears. He walks through Janie. The chair, sailing in slow motion, grows knives from its legs.

The car misses a mailbox.

It strikes the middle-aged man in the chest and head. His head is sliced clean off and it rolls around on the floor in a circle.

The car comes to rest in a shallow drainage ditch in the front yard of a tiny, unkempt house.

Janie stares at the large young man with knives for fingers. He walks to the dead man's head and kicks it like a soccer ball. It crashes loudly through the window and there is a blinding flash of light—

11:31 p.m.

Janie groans and opens her eyes. Her head is against the steering wheel. She has a cut on her lip that is bleeding. And Ethel is decidedly not level. When she can see clearly, she looks out the windows, and when she can move again, she eases her way out her door. She walks around the car, sees that it is not injured, and that she is not stuck. She shuts the hood gently, gets into the car, and backs up slowly.

When she arrives in her driveway, she breathes a sigh of relief, and then memorizes the exact location of the parking brake by feel. She sees the keys dangling from the ignition. *Duh*, she thinks.

Next time, she will be ready.

Maybe she should have bought an automatic.

She hopes to God it doesn't happen on a highway.

12:46 a.m.

Janie lies awake in bed. Scared.

In the back of her mind, she hears the distinct sound of knives sharpening. The more she tries not to think about whose dream that might have been, the more she thinks about it. She can never drive that street again.

She wonders if she will end up like her friend Miss Stubin from the nursing home, all alone.

Or dead in a car crash, because of this stupid dream curse.

August 25, 2005

Carrie brings in the mail to Janie's. Janie is wearing a T-shirt and boxer shorts. It's hot and humid.

"Schedules are here," Carrie says. "Senior year, baby! This is it!"

Excitedly, they open their schedules together. They lay them side-by-side on the coffee table and compare.

Their facial expressions go from excitement, to disappointment, and then excitement again.

"So, first period English and fifth period study hall. That's not terrible," Janie says.

"And we have the same lunch," Carrie says. "Let me see what Melinda has. I'll be right back." Carrie gets up to leave.

"You can call her from here, you know," Janie says, rolling her eyes.

"I-I would, but—"

Janie waits for Carrie to explain. Then it dawns on her. "Oh," she says. "I get it. Caller ID. Sheesh, Carrie."

Carrie looks at her shoes, then slips out.

Janie checks the freezer for ice cream. She eats it out of the carton. She feels like shit.

September 6, 2005, 7:35 a.m.

Carrie and Janie drive separately to school, because Janie has to work at 3 p.m. Janie waves from the window when she hears Carrie's car horn beep. *This is it*, she thinks.

Janie is only mildly excited to start her senior year of high school. And she is not at all excited to have study hall right after lunch.

She brushes her teeth and grabs her backpack, checking the mirror briefly before heading out the door. She is stopped by the flashing red lights of her former bus, and she smirks when she sees the noobs all climbing the steps to board it. Most of them are dressed in the styles of five years ago—hand-me-downs, or secondhand thrift clothing. "Get jobs, and get the hell out of South Fieldridge," Janie mutters. At least there's strength in numbers.

Ethel purrs.

Janie continues when the red lights stop. A block before the "bad" house on Waverly Road, she turns to take a detour. She's not taking any chances. She slows as she sees someone walking toward her along the road, wearing a ratty backpack. At first, she doesn't recognize him.

And then, she does.

He looks different.

He's not carrying a skateboard.

"You missed it," Janie says through the open window. "Get in. I'll drive you."

Cabel eyes her warily. His features have matured. He's wearing eyeglasses, the new cool rimless kind. His jaw is decidedly angular. He looks both thinner and more muscular at the same time. His hair, wavy at shoulder length, is layered slightly, no longer blue-black or greasy, but golden light brown. His long bangs that hung in his eyes last year are tucked behind his ears this year. And it looks freshly washed. He hesitates, and then opens the passenger door.

"Thanks." His voice is low and gruff. "Jesus," he remarks as he tries to fit his knees inside.

Janie reaches down between her legs. "Grab yours too," she says.

He raises an eyebrow.

"Your seat adjustor, you ass. We have to pull them together. It's a bench seat. As you can see." They pull, and the seat moves back a notch. Janie checks the clutch to make sure she can still reach. She shifts into first as Cabel shuts his door.

"You're on the wrong street," he remarks.

"I know that."

"I figured you were lost or something."

"Oh, puhleeze. I-I take a detour. I don't drive on Waverly anymore. I'm superstitious."

He glances at her and shrugs. "Whatever."

They ride in awkward silence for five minutes, until Janie rolls her eyes inwardly and says, "So. What's your schedule?"

"I have no idea."

"Okaaay . . ." The conversation fizzles.

After a moment, he opens his backpack and takes out a sealed envelope. He rips it open as if it's a chore of great difficulty and looks over his schedule.

"English, math, Spanish, industrial tech, lunch, study hall, government, P.E." He sounds bored.

Janie cringes. "Hmmm. Interesting."

"And yours?" He says it too politely, as if he is forced to chat with his grandmother.

"It's, ah . . . actually . . . ," she sighs, ". . . pretty similar to that. Yeah."

He laughs. "Don't sound so fucking excited, Hannagan. I'll let you cheat off my papers."

She smiles wryly. "Yeah, right! Like I'd want to."

He looks at her. "And your GPA is?"

"Three point eight." She sniffs.

"Well, then, of course you don't need help."

"What's yours?"

He shifts in the seat and shoves his schedule into his backpack. "I have no idea."

That was the most Cabel Strumheller had ever spoken to Janie in all the years she'd known him. Combined. Including the three miles on the skateboard.

12:45 p.m.

Janie meets up with Carrie in study hall. Seniors have study hall in the library so they can access the books and computers and hopefully do actual work rather than sleep. Janie hopes for the best and finds a table in the far corner of the room.

"How's it going?" Janie asks.

"Decent," Carrie says. "The only class I have with Melinda is English. Hey, did you see the new guy?"

"What new guy?"

"In English class."

Janie looks puzzled. "I didn't notice."

Carrie looks around sneakily. "Oh, shit!" she whispers. "Here he comes."

Janie glances up. Carrie is staring at her, not daring to turn around again. He nods in her direction. Janie waves her fingers at him. To Carrie, she says, "Oh, you mean him?"

"You did NOT just wave to him."

"To who . . . er, whom? Yeah, that's it. Whom?"

"The new guy! Aren't you listening to me?" Carrie bounces in her chair.

Janie grins innocently. "Watch this." She gets up, walks to the table where the new guy sits, and pulls up a chair across from him so she can see Carrie watching.

"I have a question for you," Janie says.

"I thought you didn't need my help," he replies, rummaging through his backpack.

"It's not that kind."

"Go ahead, then."

"Are you getting a lot of strange looks today, by any chance?"

He pulls his notebook out of his backpack, takes off his outer button-down shirt, leaving on a loose, white T-shirt. He folds the button-down haphazardly, sets it on top of his backpack, scoots his chair back, and lays his head on the shirt. His newly muscular arms reach around this makeshift pillow.

"I hadn't noticed," he says. He takes off his glasses and sets them off to the side.

Janie nods thoughtfully. "I see. So . . . you don't know what classes you have, you don't know your GPA, you don't notice all the girls drooling over your new look—"

"That's bullshit," he says, closing his eyes.

"So what do you pay attention to?"

He opens his eyes. Lifts his head from his pillow. He looks at Janie for a long time. His eyes are silky brown. She's never noticed them before.

For a split second, Janie thinks she sees something in them, but then it's gone.

"Pfft. You wouldn't believe me if I told you," he says.

Janie flashes a crooked smile, shrugs, and shakes her head slightly, feeling warm. "Try me."

Cabel raises a skeptical eyebrow.

"You know . . . sometime," she says finally. She picks up his shirt and refolds it so the buttons turn in. "So you don't get a button impression on your face," she says.

"Thank you," he says. His eyes don't leave hers. He's searching them. His brow furrows.

Janie clears her throat lightly. "So, uh, shall I break the news to Carrie that you're not a new guy?"

Cabel blinks. "What?"

"Half the girls in the school think you're a new student. Cabel, come on. You look a lot different from last year. . . ."

The words trail off her tongue and they sound wrong.

He gives her a confused look.

"What did you call me?"

Janie's stomach lurches. "Um, Cabel?"

He isn't smiling. "Who do you think I am?"

Maybe she's in somebody's weird dream and she doesn't know it.

She panics.

"Oh, God, no," she whispers. She stands up abruptly and tries to get past him. He catches her arm.

"Whoa, time out," he says. "Sit."

Tears pool in Janie's eyes. She covers her mouth.

"Jesus, Janie. I'm just playing with your mind a little. I'm sorry. Hey," he says. He keeps hold of her wrist, lightly.

She feels like a fool.

"Come on, Hannagan. Look at me, will you? Listen to me."

Janie can't look at him. She sees Carrie, half-standing, peering over the bookshelves, a concerned look on her face. Janie waves her away. Carrie sits down.

"Janie."

"What, already," she says, growing hot. "And will you please let go of me before I call security?"

He drops her wrist like a baked potato.

His eyes widen.

"Forget it." He sighs. "I'm an asshole." He looks away.

Janie walks back to her table and sits down miserably.

"What was that?" Carrie hisses.

Janie looks at her and summons a calm smile. She shakes her head. "Nothing. The new guy just told me . . . that . . ." She stalls, pretending to search for a pen. "That, uh, I'm doing the advance math equations completely wrong. I . . . you know me. I hate to be wrong. Math's my best subject, you know." She pulls out a sheet of paper and opens her math book. "Now I've got to start all over."

"Sheesh, Janie. You looked like he just threatened to kill you or something."

Janie laughs. "As if."

1:30 p.m.

Cabel tries to catch Janie's eye in government class. She ignores him.

2:20 p.m.

P.E. It's coed this year. The students play rotating games of five-on-five basketball. Guys against the girls.

Janie commits the most egregious foul Fieldridge High School has ever seen. When he is able, the new guy stands up and insists it was his fault.

The P.E. staff confer, and decide girls versus guys is not a good idea for contact sports. Coach Crater gives Janie a hard look. She returns it, with interest.

2:45 p.m.

Janie dries off hurriedly after her shower and slips into her scrubs for work. The bell rings. She takes her stuff and jumps in her car so she's not late for work.

8:01 p.m.

Life is blissfully calm at Heather Home tonight. Janie finishes her paperwork and her other duties on the floor early, so she goes to see Miss Stubin. She shuffles her feet and clears her throat so Miss Stubin knows Janie is there.

"It's me, Janie. Are you up for a few chapters of *Jane Eyre*?" Janie asks.

Miss Stubin smiles warmly and turns her face toward Janie's voice. "I'd love it, if you have the time."

Janie pulls the visitor chair closer to the bed and begins where they left off last time. She doesn't notice when Miss Stubin drifts off to sleep.

8:24 p.m.

Janie is standing on a street called Center in a small town. Everything is in black and white, like an old movie. Nearby, a couple strolls arm and arm, window-shopping. Janie follows them. The store windows are filled with simplicity. Saws and hammers. Yarn and material. Baking sheets and metal tins. Dry goods.

The couple stops at the corner, and Janie can see the young woman has been crying. The young man is wearing a military uniform.

He pulls the young woman gently around the corner of the building, and they kiss passionately. He touches her breast and says something, and she shakes her head, no. He tries again, and she moves his hand away. He pulls back. "Please, Martha. Let me make love to you before I go."

The young woman, Martha, begins to say no. Then she turns, and looks at Janie with complete regret in her eyes. "Not even in my dream?" she says.

Martha waits for Janie to respond.

Janie looks at the young man. He is frozen, momentarily,

gazing adoringly at Martha. Martha pleads with her eyes locked on Janie. "Help me, Janie."

Janie, startled, shrugs and nods, and Martha smiles through her tears. She turns back to the young man, touches his face, his lips, and nods. They walk through the alley, away from Janie. Janie takes a step to follow them, but she doesn't want to see any more of this dream—it's too intimate. She grips the chair in Miss Stubin's room with all her might, concentrates, and pulls herself back into the nursing home.

It's 8:43 p.m. Janie shakes her head to clear it. Surprised. Slowly, a grin spreads across her face. She did it—she pulled herself out of the dream. And she's not getting sucked back into it. Janie chuckles quietly to herself.

Miss Stubin sleeps peacefully, a smile on her thin, tired lips. It must be nice for poor old Miss Stubin to have a good dream.

Janie leaves the book on the table and exits the room quietly. She turns off the light and closes the door, giving Miss Stubin some intimate time alone with her soldier.

Before he dies.

And she never has the chance again.

September 9, 2005, 12:45 p.m.

"Why didn't you tell me the new guy was Cabel Strumheller?" Carrie demands.

Janie looks up from her book. She sits in the library at their usual table. "Because I'm an asshole?" She smiles sweetly.

Carrie tries to hold back a laugh. "Yes, you are. I see you're driving him to school."

"Only when he misses the bus," Janie says lightly.

Carrie gives her a sly smile. "Yeah, well. Anyways, I made yearbook staff, so I'll be gone a lot during study hall, okay? I gotta go there now for the first meeting."

Janie waves, distracted by the play she's reading for English. "Have fun. Play nice." She slides down in her seat and plops her feet on the chair opposite hers. She's reading *Camelot* in preparation for next month's senior English trip to Stratford, Canada.

Every now and then she peers over the bookshelves to see if anyone is looking sleepy nearby. She figures she can handle anything outside a twenty-foot radius, unless it's a nightmare, and then the distance jumps dramatically. Luckily, most school-day dreams tend to either be the "falling" dream, the "naked presentation" dream, or something sexual. She can usually get a handle on those without doing a full pass-out-on-the-floor reaction.

It's the paralyzing, shiver-and-shake nightmares that are killing her.

12:55 p.m.

The book disappears in front of her. Janie sighs and sets it on the table. She lays her head in her arms and closes her eyes.

She is floating. *Not the falling dream again,* she thinks. She is sick to death of the falling dream.

The scene changes immediately. Now, Janie is outside. It's dark. She's alone, behind a shed, but she can hear muffled voices. She's never been alone before, and she doesn't know how people can have dreams that they are not in. She is curious. She watches nervously, hoping this isn't somebody's nightmare about to explode through the wall of the shed, or from the bushes.

From around the corner comes a hulking, monstrous figure, outlined by the moonlight. It thrashes its arms through the bushes and lifts its hands to the sky, letting out a horrible yell. Janie feels her fingers going numb. She tries to get out. But she can't.

The figure's long fingers glint in the moonlight.

Janie leans back against the barn. She is shaking.

The grotesque figure sharpens his knife-fingers on each other. The sound is deafening.

Janie, against the barn, squeaks.

The figure wheels around. He sees her.

Approaches her.

She has seen this character before.

Right before she and Ethel ended up in a ditch.

Janie stands up, tries to run. But her legs won't move.

The figure's face is furious, but he has stopped sharpening his knives. He's five feet away, and Janie closes her eyes. *Nothing can hurt me,* she tries to tell herself.

When she opens her eyes, it is daylight. She is still behind the barn. And the horrid, menacing figure has turned into a normal, human young man.

It's Cabel Strumheller.

A second Janie steps out from Janie's body and walks to Cabel, unafraid.

Janie stays back, against the barn.

Cabel touches the second Janie's face.

He leans in.

He kisses her.

She kisses him back.

He steps out of the embrace and looks at the Janie against the barn wall. Tears fall down his cheeks.

"Help me," he says.

1:35 p.m.

The bell rings. Janie feels the fog lifting, but she cannot move. Not yet. She needs a minute.

1:36 p.m.

Make that two minutes.

1:37 p.m.

When she feels the hand on her shoulder, she jumps.

A mile, a foot, an inch . . . she doesn't know.

She looks up.

"Ready?" he says. "Didn't know if you heard the bell."

She stares at him.

"You okay, Hannagan?"

She nods and grabs her books. "Yeah." Her voice is not completely back yet. She clears her throat. "Yes," she says firmly. "Are you? You have a dent in your cheek." She smiles shakily.

"Fell asleep on my book."

"I figured."

"You too, huh?"

"I, uh, must've been really tired, I guess."

"You look freaked. Did you have a bad dream or something?"

She looks at him as they walk through the crowded hall to government class. He slips his hand onto the small of her back so they stay together as they talk.

"Not exactly," she says slowly. Her eyes narrow. "Did you?" The words come out of her mouth like gunshots.

He turns sharply into the doorway as the bell rings and he sees the look on her face. He stops in his tracks. His eyes narrow as they search her face. She can see his eyes are puzzled. His face flushes slightly, but she's not sure why.

The teacher comes in and shoos them to their seats.

Janie looks over her shoulder, two rows back and toward the middle of the room.

Cabel is still staring at her, looking incredibly puzzled. He shakes his head just slightly.

She looks at the chalkboard. Not seeing it. Just wondering. Wondering what the hell is wrong with her. And what is wrong with *him*, that he has dreams like that. Does he know? Did he see her in that one?

2:03 p.m.

A wad of paper lands on Janie's desk. She jumps and slowly looks over to Cabel. He is slumped in his seat, doodling on his notebook, looking a little too innocent.

Janie opens the paper.

Smooths it out.

Yeah, maybe . . . (?)

That's what it says.

September 29, 2005 2:55 p.m.

Leaning against the hood of her car is the lanky, long-haired figure of Cabel Strumheller. The one who dreams about monsters, and kissing her all in the same dream. His hair is wet.

"Hey," Janie says lightly. Her hair is wet too.

"Why are you avoiding me?"

She sighs. "Am I?" She knows it sounds fake.

He doesn't answer.

She gets in the car.

Starts the engine.

Pulls out of the parking space.

Cabel stands there, looking. Arms folded across his chest. His lips are concerned.

She leans over and rolls down the window. "Get in. You've missed the bus by now."

His expression doesn't change.

He doesn't move.

She hesitates, one more minute.

He turns and starts walking toward home.

She watches him, sighs exasperatedly, and guns it. Her tires squeal around the corner. *Idiot.*

October 10, 2005, 4:57 a.m.

On a thin piece of paper in the cave of her own dream, Janie writes:

I keep to myself.

I have to.

Because of what I know about you.

And then she crumples it up, lights a match, and turns it into ash. The charcoaled remains shrivel up and the wind takes them down the street, across the yards. To his house. He steps on them as he saunters to catch the bus. The ash is softer than the crisp Halloween leaves that gather and huddle around the corners of his front step. Under the weight of his footstep, the ash disintegrates. The wind swallows it. Gone.

7:15 a.m.

Janie wakes up, running late for school. She blinks.

She has never had a dream before—not that she can remember.

She only has everyone else's.

At least she can sleep during hers.

She gives her straight dirty-blond hair a lesson with a wet comb, brushes her teeth at top speed, shoves two dollars in the front pocket of her jeans, and grabs her backpack, searching wildly for her keys. They are on the kitchen table. She grabs them, saying good-bye to her nightgowned mother, who stands at the sink eating a Pop-Tart and looking aimlessly out the window.

"I'm late," Janie says.

Her mother doesn't respond.

Janie lets the door slam, but not angrily. Hurriedly. She climbs into the Nova and zooms to Fieldridge High School. She's ten long strides from her English classroom when the bell rings, just like half the class. Sliding into her desk, the back seat in the row nearest the door, she mouses unnoticed through the class, except for a sleepy grin from Carrie. Janie stealthily finishes her math assignment as the teacher drones about the upcoming weekend senior trip to Stratford.

Cabel's back is to her. She has an urge to touch his hair. If she could reach him, she might. But then she shakes her head at herself. She is very confused over her feelings about him. It's more bizarre than flattering to know he dreams about her. Especially when he does it after being that horrid monster-man. She may even admit to being a little afraid of him.

And now she knows where he lives.

Just two blocks from her.

In a tiny house on Waverly Road.

"Your room assignments," Mr. Purcell drones, waving fluorescent yellow papers like sun rays above his head before tossing handfuls at the first person in each row. “No changes allowed, so don’t even try.”

Janie looks up as titters and groans fill the room. The boy in front of her doesn’t turn around to hand her the paper. He tosses it over his shoulder. It floats, hovers, and slides off the slick laminate desk before Janie can grab it, whooshing and sticking under Cabel Strumheller’s shoe. He kicks it toward her without acknowledgment. His hair swings lightly around his shoulders.

The list places Janie in a room with three rich snobs from the ritzy Hill section of North Fieldridge: Melinda Jeffers, who hates her, Melinda’s friend Shay Wilder, who hates her by default, and the captain of the girls’ soccer team, Savannah Jackson, who pretends Janie doesn’t exist. She sighs inwardly. She’ll have to sleep on the bus on the way.

But she’s curious to know if, after all these years, Melinda still dreams about Carrie with ginormous boobs.

OH, CANADA

October 14, 2005, 3:30 a.m.

Janie meets Carrie under the black sky in Carrie's driveway. They offer little greeting besides sleepy grins, and Janie climbs into the passenger seat of Carrie's Tracer. They drive in silent darkness to school. Janie's just glad she doesn't have to drive at this hour.

They pass Cabel Strumheller when they get close to school. He's walking. Carrie slows and stops, rolls down the window, and asks if he wants a ride, but he waves her off with a grin. "I'm almost there," he says. Up ahead, the Greyhound bus gleams under the school's parking lot lights.

Janie looks at Cabel. He catches her eye briefly and looks down. She feels like shit.

Cabel and Janie's non-fight in the parking lot began a long series of non-fights. Not only do they not fight, they no longer speak.

But Janie sees him, kisses him, in his library dreams.

She also sees him, a raging maniac. A scarred-faced lunatic with knife-fingers, who repetitively stabs, slices, and beheads one middle-aged man, over and over and over again. She feels only slight relief that he doesn't kill anyone else.

Not yet, anyway.

Not her, so far.

And every time he dreams it, the bell rings before Janie can figure out how to help him. Help him do what? Help him, how?

She has no idea. She has no power. Why do all these people ask her for help? She can't do it.

Just.

Can't.

Do it.

But she sure doesn't get much done in study hall these days.

3:55 a.m.

The oversleepers, latecomers, and don't-give-a-shitters

have either arrived or been written off by the teacher chaperones. Carrie sits with Melinda, near the front.

Janie sits in the last row on the right, next to the window. As far away from everyone as she can get. She stows her overnight bag in the compartment above her seat. She is glad to note that the restroom is at the front of the bus. She twists the overhead TV monitor so its blue glow doesn't blind her, and puts her seat back. It only goes a little way before it hits the back wall.

Before the bus is loaded, Janie is dozing.

4:35 a.m.

She is jarred awake by a splash of water in her face. She's in a lake, fully clothed. She shivers. A boy named Kyle is yelling as he falls from the sky above her, over and over and over, until he finally lands in the water. But he can't swim. Janie feels her fingers growing numb, and she kicks out with her feet, trying to stop it, trying to get out.

And then it's done.

Janie blinks, and sits up, startled. A shadowy face appears above the seat in front of her. "What the fuck?" says Kyle. "Do you mind?"

"Sorry," Janie whispers. Her heart races. The drowning dreams are the worst. Well, almost.

She hears a whisper in her ear as she struggles to see

clearly. "You okay, Hannagan?" Cabel slips his arm around her. He sounds worried. "You're shivering. Did you just have a seizure or something? You want me to stop the bus?"

Janie looks at him. "Oh, hey." Her voice is scratchy. "I didn't know you were there. Um . . ." She closes her eyes. Tries to think. Holds up a weak finger, letting him know she needs a moment. But she feels the next one coming already. She doesn't have much time. And she has to prepare him. She doesn't have a choice.

"Cabel. Do not freak if—when—I do that again, okay? Do NOT stop the bus. Do NOT tell a teacher, oh God, no. No matter what." She grips the armrests and fights to keep her vision. "Can you trust me? Trust me and just let it happen?"

The pain of concentration is excruciating. She is cringing, holding her head. "Oh, fuckity-fuck!" she yells in a whisper. "This was a stupid, stupid idea for me to come on this trip. Please, Cabel. Help me. Don't let . . . anyone . . . gah! . . . see me."

Cabel is gawking at Janie. "Okay," he says. "Okay. Jesus."

But she is gone.

The dreams pelt her, from all directions, without ceasing. Janie is on sensory overload. It's her own physical, mental, emotional, three-hour nightmare.

7:48 a.m.

Janie opens her eyes. Someone is talking on a microphone.

When the fog fades and she can see again, finally, Cabel is staring at her. His eyes, his hair, are wild. His face is white. He is holding her around the shoulders.

Gripping her, is more like it.

She feels like crying, and she does, a little. She closes her eyes and doesn't move. Can't move. The tears leak out. Cabel wipes her cheeks gently with his thumb.

That makes her cry harder.

8:15 a.m.

The bus stops. They are parked in a McDonald's parking lot. Everyone files off the bus. Everyone except Janie and Cabel.

"Go get some food," she urges in a tired whisper. Her voice is still not back.

"No."

"Seriously. I'll be okay, now that everyone's . . . gone."

"Janie."

"Will you go and get me a breakfast sandwich then?" She's still breathing hard. "I need to eat. Something. Anything. There's money in my right-hand coat pocket." The effort to move her arm seems too difficult.

Cabel looks at her. His eyes are weary. Bleary. He

removes his glasses and pinches the bridge of his nose, then rubs his eyes. He sighs deeply. "You sure you'll be okay? I'll be back in five minutes or less." He looks unwilling to leave her.

She smiles a tired half smile. "I'll be fine. Please. I don't think I can stand up if I don't get something to eat soon. That was much, much worse than I expected."

He hesitates, and then removes his arm from behind her shoulders. "I'll be back." He sprints off the bus. She watches him out the window. He runs through the empty drive-through lane and taps on the microphone. Janie smiles. What a dork.

He returns with a bag full of breakfast sandwiches, several orders of hash browns, coffee, orange juice, milk, and a chocolate shake. "I wasn't sure what you'd want," he says.

Janie struggles a little and sits up. She pours the juice down her throat and swallows until it's gone. She does the same with the milk.

"Can you chug beer like that?"

She smiles, grateful he isn't asking questions about her strange behavior. "I've never tried it with beer."

"That's probably wise."

"Have you?" She takes a bite of a sandwich.

"I don't really drink."

"Not even a little, here and there?"

"Nope."

She looks at him. "I thought you were a partier. Drugs?"

He hesitates a split second. "Nada."

"Wow. Well, you sure looked like hell for a couple years."

He is quiet. He smiles politely. "Thank you." He nods at her sandwich.

"Sorry."

He stares at the seat in front of them while she eats. She hands him a sandwich and he takes it, unwraps it, and eats it slowly. They sit in silence.

Janie belches loudly.

He looks at her. Grins. "Jesus, Hannagan. You should enter a contest."

They share the chocolate shake.

8:35 a.m.

The other students board the bus in twos and threes. Some stand outside, sucking on cigarettes.

8:41 a.m.

The bus begins to move again.

"Now what?" asks Cabel. He has a look of concern around his eyes. He combs his hair with his fingers, and it feathers and falls again.

"If it happens again, don't worry." She shrugs helplessly.

"I don't know what to tell you—I promise I'll explain this all when I can. Where are we, by the way?"

"We're getting close."

She rummages around in her pocket and produces a ten-dollar bill. "For breakfast," she says.

He shakes his head and pushes it away. "Let me think of this as our first date, will you?"

She looks at him for a long moment. Feels her stomach flip. "Okay," she whispers.

He touches her cheek. "You look exhausted. Can you sleep?"

"Until somebody else does, I suppose."

His eyes turn weary again. "What does that mean, Janie?" He puts his arm around her shoulders. She rests her head against him and doesn't answer. In minutes, she is sleeping gently. He takes her hand with his free hand and strings his fingers in hers. Looks at her hands, and lays his cheek against her hair. After a while, he is asleep too.

9:16 a.m.

Janie is outside, in the dark. She looks behind her, and the shed is there. She walks around the shed this time, to see him coming.

He looks normal—not a monster—standing at the back door of a house, looking in. Then he slams the door and marches through the dry, yellow grass. The middle-aged man bursts out the door after him, yelling, standing on the step. He carries a rectangular can in one hand, a beer and a cigarette in the other. He screams at Cabel. Cabel turns to face him. The man charges, and Cabel stands there, frozen. Waiting for the man to approach him.

The man punches Cabel in the face and he goes down. He squirms on his back like a scared crab, trying to get away. The man points and squeezes the rectangular can, and liquid hits Cabel's shorts and shirt.

Then.

The man flicks his cigarette at Cabel.

Cabel ignites.

Flops around on the ground in flames.

Screaming, like a poor, tortured baby bunny.

And then Cabel transforms. He becomes a monster, and the fire is gone. His fingers grow knives. His body grows like the Hulk.

Janie watches all this from around the corner of the shed. She doesn't want to see it. No more of it. Feeling so sick, so horrible for witnessing it. She turns around abruptly.

Standing behind her, watching her in horror, is Cabel.

The second.

9:43 a.m.

Janie waits an eternity for her sight to clear. For the feeling to come back. She sits up, frantic. She reaches for him.

Cabel is leaning over, his head in his hands.

He is shaking.

He turns to her, his face enraged.

His voice is raspy. "What the fuck is wrong with you!?"

Janie doesn't know what to say.

His silent anger shakes the seats.

10:05 a.m.

Cabel doesn't speak until they arrive in Stratford. And then all he says is a harsh "good luck." He gets off the bus and heads for his hotel room.

Janie watches him go.

She closes her eyes, then opens them again, and follows the cheerleaders in the other direction to their room.

Once inside, they don't acknowledge one another.

Janie's quite good with that.

2:00 p.m.

The students meet in the lobby. *Camelot* starts in thirty minutes. Janie boards the bus, exhausted, and sits in the back row again.

Cabel doesn't show up.

2:33 p.m.

The play begins. Janie excuses herself from her orchestra seat and finds a spot in the near-empty balcony.

She sleeps soundly up there for three hours, awaking in the closing scene. She slips back down to the orchestra seats and follows the others back to the bus.

6:01 p.m.

The bus stops at Pizza Hut. They have one hour to eat before going back to the evening play.

Janie grabs a Personal Pan to go, eats it on the bus, and sleeps. Sleeps right through the play, in her backseat spot. Nobody seems to notice she didn't get off the bus.

11:33 p.m.

The bus arrives, most kids exhausted, back at the hotel. Janie falls into bed. She is numb, but not from anyone's dream. Not this time. She thinks about Cabel. Cries silently in her pillow in the dark room. The heat register hums loudly. Savannah, the captain of the women's soccer team, collapses on the covers next to her. They don't speak. They hover at the edges of their bed.

October 15, 2005, 1:04 a.m.–6:48 a.m.

Janie jumps from one dream to another.

Savannah dreams about making the U.S. women's soccer team, and meeting the legendary Mia Hamm, even though she's retired. Big surprise—this dream could totally be an episode of *Lizzie McGuire*. Just when Janie wonders if Savannah has even the slightest bit of depth to her, Savannah's dream turns to Kyle, who sat in front of Janie on the bus. Interesting combo, there. Janie's intrigued.

Until the switch to Melinda.

Melinda, no surprise, has a three-way sex party going on with Shay Wilder, who is in bed next to her, and with Carrie. The sex is normal at first, then unbelievably tacky, in Janie's opinion. The bodies of Carrie and Shay are, to use a crass phrase, blown out of proportion. Janie manages for the first time in someone else's dream to turn away.

Janie counts it as a major victory.

And then there's Shay.

Shay dreams about Cabel Strumheller.

A lot.

And in a lot of different ways.

By morning, Janie hates Shay with all her heart. And she has very dark circles under her eyes.

8:08 a.m.

Shay, Melinda, and Savannah head down to breakfast. The matinee is at 10:00.

"See you on the bus," Janie says, even though she is starving. The other girls don't bother to answer. Janie rolls her eyes.

She takes a shower, wraps a towel around her head, and falls back into the bed. She sets the alarm for noon. The bus will be back for the luggage, and the students who didn't elect to take in a third play, at 1 p.m.

8:34 a.m.

Janie dreams for the second time in her life. She dreams that she is alone, drowning in a dark lake, and Cabel is on the shore with a rope, but he won't throw it to her. She waves frantically to him, and he can't see her. She slips under the water slowly. Under the water, she sees others like her. Babies, children, teens, adults. All of them floating just under the surface of the water, no one able to help.

It's because they're all dead.

Their eyes bulge.

She is screaming when the alarm goes off. Her towel has fallen off her head, and her hair is in tangles. She can't see beyond it.

There is an urgent knock on the door.

And it's him.

He's holding a bag of food.

Looking mournful.

He pushes past her into the room, closes the door and locks it, takes her hand, and holds her. He is pleading. "I don't understand," he says. "I just don't understand. Why did you do that to me?" He's broken.

And so is she. "I can explain," Janie says. And she buries her face in his shirt and cries. "Just get me home."

They fall on the bed, and they just hold each other quietly.

That's all they do.

And then, it's time to go home.

2:00 p.m.

Janie and Cabel are in the back seats again. Carrie and Melinda sit in front of them. Across the aisle, Savannah and Kyle are making out. Janie reminds herself to start taking bets on these things.

In front of Savannah and Kyle is Shay, or at least her baggage. Shay appears to be furiously ignoring Janie. She tries to strike up a conversation with Cabel by sitting on the aisle floor, next to him. Cabel is cool and mildly disinterested.

This makes Shay try harder.

Carrie and Melinda turn around in their seats to chat. Cabel makes small talk and jokes, while Janie looks out the window. He slips his hand into hers.

The other girls notice.

Carrie winks.

Melinda looks at Carrie with burning eyes.

Shay shifts in the aisle and leans against Cabel's leg, batting her eyelashes madly. Frighteningly.

At the front of the bus, kids are roaming around and laughing, singing, chattering. Awake and buzzing. Janie slips into a grateful coma, her head propped against the window.

7:31 p.m.

They are back at Fieldridge High School. Cabel shakes Janie awake, gently. She sits up, wondering where she is. Cabel grins at her. "You made it," he whispers. He gathers their bags and follows her off the bus. He walks with her to Carrie's car.

"Come on, Cabel," Carrie says. "Let me give you a ride, at least. Unless you want Shay to—hey, here she comes now." Carrie titters, her eyes dancing.

Cabel's eyes grow wide. He slips into the backseat of Carrie's car without a word. "Get me outta here. Fuckin' creepy cheerleaders."

Carrie laughs. She pulls out of the parking lot and eases onto the road ahead of the pack, and turns to Cabel. "So where do you live?"

"Waverly. Two blocks straight east of your house. But I'll walk from Janie's, if you don't mind. Janie has a superstition about my street."

"What the hell?" Carrie snorts.

Janie laughs. "Nothing! Shut up, Cabe."

Carrie pulls into her driveway. It's cool outside. Crisp. The harvest moon shines orange on Ethel's roof in the Hannagan driveway. Carrie grabs her things and yawns. "I'm turning in. Catch you guys later." She clops to her front door and lets herself in, waving as she closes the screen door.

Janie takes her bag and waves to Carrie. She looks at Cabel. It feels awkward, now that they are in Janie's front yard. They walk to her door. "Can you come in for a bit?" Janie asks, trying not to sound anxious.

"Sure," he says, his voice relieved. "I, uh, figure we have some things to talk about. Are the 'rents home?"

"My mother's probably passed out in her bedroom. That's it, just me and her."

"Cool," he says, but he gives her an understanding look.

They go inside. There is no sign of Janie's mother, except for an empty fifth of vodka on the kitchen counter and a sink full of dishes. Janie throws the bottle in the trash. "Sorry about the mess," she says in a low voice. She is embarrassed. The house was spotless when she left it yesterday morning.

"Forget about it. We can clean it up later, if you want."

Janie waves her hand at the living room. "Well. This is it," she says.

"You sleep out here, huh?" He isn't teasing.

"No, I have a bedroom. Come." She shows him. It's sparse and neat.

"Nice," he says. He glances at the bed, and then abruptly turns around and they walk back to the living room.

"Hungry?"

"My stomach's growling," he says.

"Let me see if we have anything." Janie searches the kitchen cupboards and refrigerator and comes up empty-handed. "Good grief," she says finally. "I'm sorry." She turns around. "We got nothin'."

He's been watching her, she realizes.

"Maybe we could get a pizza."

"Sounds good."

"You want to go out?"

Janie sighs and scratches her head. "Not really."

"Good. Let's order delivery."

Janie finds the number for Fred's Pizza and Grinders and orders. "Thirty minutes."

Cabel tosses a twenty-dollar bill on the coffee table and sits down.

"Cabe."

"Yes."

"What is that?"

"It's twenty dollars, Hannagan."

Janie sighs. "Let's be truthful with each other here, mmmkay?"

"Of course. Our whole relationship is based on it. Right?" He's smiling sardonically, and looks down.

She cringes as the words hang ominously in the room. "Look, I'm sorry," she begins. "I have a lot of explaining to do. But I know you don't have any more money to spare than I do. So how about I pay for this?"

"No. Next question."

Janie sits down next to him. Shakes her head. "Fine," she says, giving up. She draws her legs up under her and turns to face him.

"Okay," she continues. "How did you get in the dream twice?"

He looks away, and then back to Janie.

"Well, let's just jump right into it, then."

"I guess."

"All right . . . uh . . . I guess the answer is, I have No. Fucking. Clue. Oh, and just let me know when it's my turn to ask a few questions. Because I'd like to know how the hell you. Got into. My dream. Hello."

Janie blushes. "Some of your dreams are kind of great."

"Oh, really." Cabel leans forward and catches her chin. Catches her by surprise. He pulls her toward him and traces her cheekbone with his thumb. And then, he puts his lips on hers.

Janie falls into the kiss. She closes her eyes and slips her hand to his shoulder. They explore the kiss for a moment, sweetly. Cabel digs his fingers into her hair and he pulls her closer. But before it grows any stronger, Janie pulls away. She feels like her limbs are rubber.

"Shit," she sputters. "You . . . you . . ."

He smiles lazily, his lips still wet. "Yes?"

"You kiss better than I imagined. Even in—"

He blinks. "No," he says. "No, no, no. Don't even tell me you've been there."

She bites her lip. "Well, maybe if you stopped sleeping during study hall, I wouldn't have a clue."

"Good God!" he says. "Is nothing sacred? Sheesh." He turns away, embarrassed. "Maybe you should start from the beginning."

Janie sighs and leans back against the couch. It was like reliving the dreams. Again.

"The short version? I get sucked into people's dreams. I can't help it. I can't stop it. It's driving me crazy."

He gives her a long look. "Okay, um, how? That's just bizarre."

"I don't know."

"Is this a recent thing?"

"No. The first one I remember, I was eight."

"So, in that dream, *my* dream, where I'm standing behind you, watching myself . . . in . . ." He holds his head. "Okay, so that's how you see the dreams, right? Like I saw mine. While I was dreaming it. Ughh." He rubs his temples.

"That was weird, huh," Janie says softly. "I know this is all really weird. I'm sorry."

There's a knock at the door. Janie jumps up, relieved. She grabs the twenty and goes to answer it.

She sets the pizza and a two-liter of Pepsi on the coffee table and goes to the kitchen for a beer, glasses, napkins, and paper plates. She pours the Pepsi for Cabel and clips open the beer. She takes a sip as Cabel grabs some pizza.

"Now. Tell me what else you've seen in my dreams, before I get really paranoid."

"Okay," she says, suddenly feeling a bit shy. She takes another sip and begins. "We're behind that shed or barn of some sort. Is that your backyard?"

He nods, chewing.

"Up until yesterday, I've seen you as the monster-man-thing"—she cringes, not sure what to name it—"that monster in the house—the kitchen. With the chair. That one was purely coincidental—I didn't even know it was you, dreaming it. Not until later. It was sort of a drive-by thing."

He closes his eyes, cringes, and sets his pizza down on the plate.

"That was you," he says slowly. "I knew I'd seen your car before. I thought you were . . . someone else." He pauses, lost in thought. "The yard—oh, God—your so-called superstition. Damn. So—" He sits up, hands paused in midair, eyes closed. Thinking. Processing.

And then he turns and stares at her. "You could have totally crashed."

"I didn't think anybody saw me."

"The headlights—your headlights. That's what woke me up. They were shining in my window. . . . Jesus Christ, Janie."

"Your bedroom window must have been open. Otherwise, it wouldn't have happened. I think. I had no idea it was your house."

He sits back, shaking his head slightly as he puts the pieces together. "Okay," he says. "Get to the good part before I completely lose my appetite."

"Behind the shed. You walk up to me. Touch my face. Kiss me. I kiss you back."

He's silent.

"That's it," she says.

He regards her carefully. "That's it?"

"Yes. I swear. I mean, it was a good kiss, though."

He nods, lost in thought. "Damn bell always rings then, doesn't it."

She smiles. "Yeah." She pauses, wondering if she should mention the part where he asks her to help him, but he's on to the next thing.

"So when I found you on the desk in the library a few weeks ago, and it took you a while to sit up . . . what was that? You weren't asleep, were you."

"No."

"That was a bad one?"

"Yeah. Real bad."

He puts his head in his hands and takes off his glasses. He rubs his eyes. "Jesus," he says. "I remember that one." He keeps his head down, and Janie waits. "So that's why you said . . . when I asked you if you had a bad dream," he murmurs.

"I . . . I wanted to know if you knew I was there, watching. Even when people talk to me in their dreams, no one seems to remember that part. No one ever mentions it, anyway."

"I don't recall ever seeing you there, or talking to you . . . except when I'm actually dreaming about you," he muses. "Janie," he says abruptly. "What if I don't want you to see it?"

Janie grabs a slice of pizza. "I'm working hard, trying

to bust my way out of them—the dreams. I don't want to be a voyeur—seriously, I can't help it. It's almost impossible. So far, anyway. But I'm making a little progress. Slowly." She pauses. "If you don't want me to see, I guess, don't sleep in the same room as me."

He looks up at her with a sly smile. "But I'm known for sleeping in school. It's my shtick."

"You can change your schedule. Or I can change mine. I'll do whatever you want." She looks at the uneaten pizza and sets her plate down. She is miserable.

"Whatever I want," he says.

"Yes."

"I'm afraid you haven't been privy to that dream yet."

She looks at him. He's looking at her, and she grows warm. "Maybe I'd rather experience that firsthand," she says lightly.

"Mmmm." He takes a sip of his soda. "But before this goes offtrack . . . What the hell is wrong with you?"

She's silent. Not looking at him.

"And," he says, "Jesus. It just occurred to me why you freaked when I pretended I wasn't me. You must be a freaking mess, Hannagan." He tugs her arm, and she falls back on the couch toward him. He kisses the top of her head. "I can't begin to tell you how bad I felt about that."

"It's cool," she says. "Sorry about the flagrant foul," she adds.

"S'all right. I was wearing a cup." He twirls a strand of her hair with his finger. "So, when do you sleep, like, normally?"

Janie smiles ruefully. "Normally, I sleep fine, if I'm alone in a room. When I was thirteen, I finally asked my mother if she would do me the favor of passing out in her bedroom rather than in here. There's something about a closed door that blocks it." She pauses.

"But what happens, exactly?"

She closes her eyes. "My vision goes first. I can't see around me. I'm trapped. If it's a bad dream, a nightmare, I guess I start to shake and my fingers go numb first, then my feet, and the worse the nightmare is, the more paralyzed I become."

He looks at her. "Janie," he says softly.

"Yes."

He strokes her hair. "I thought you were dying. You shake, you spasm, your eyes roll back in your head. I was ready to steal the nearest cell phone, stick a wallet in your mouth, and call 911."

Janie is silent for a long time. "It's not as bad as it looks."

"You're lying."

She looks at him. "Yes," she says. "I suppose I am."

"Who else knows? Your mother?"

She looks at her plate of uneaten pizza. Shakes her head. "Nobody. Not even her."

"You haven't been to a doctor about it or anything?"

"No. Not really. Not for help."

He throws his hands in the air. "Why?" His voice is incredulous. And then, suddenly, he knows why. "Sorry," he says.

She doesn't answer. She's thinking. Thinking hard.

"You know, nobody's ever gone there with me, like you did." Her voice is soft, musing. She gives him a sidelong glance. "I don't understand that part. How did you get there too?"

"I don't know. All of a sudden it was like I had two different angles to watch from: one of them as an observer, the other as a participant. Like virtual reality picture-in-picture or something."

"And don't even tell me you'd believe a word of this if you hadn't come through it with me."

He nods soberly. "You're right, Hannagan."

It's 10:21 p.m. when Cabel says good night at the door. He leans against the frame, and Janie kisses him lightly on the lips.

He hops off the step and starts walking home, but turns back in the driveway. "Hey, can I see you tomorrow night? Sometime around nine or ten?"

She nods, smiling. "I'll be here. Just let yourself in—Carrie always does too. It's cool."

TRUTH OR DARE

October 16, 2005, 9:30 p.m.

It's Sunday. The house is clean. Janie had the day off. She ran out for groceries in the morning, vacuumed, dusted, washed, polished, shined, and steam-cleaned.

Now, Janie is asleep on the couch.

Cabel doesn't come.

Or call.

11:47 p.m.

She sighs, clicks off the lamp, and goes to bed, miserable.

October 17, 2005 7:35 a.m.

Janie grabs her backpack and heads out the door. She's pissed. And hurt. She thinks she knows why he didn't show up.

On Ethel's windshield is a note, under the wiper. It's wet with dew.

I'm sorry,

it says.

Cabe.

Yeah, well. Not as sorry as I am, she thinks.

She passes him on the way to school.

He looks up.

And eats her dust.

He's late for school.

She doesn't speak to him.

11:19 p.m.

He's sitting on her front step.

She's pulling up to the house after work.

She gets out of the car, crunches over the gravel, and stands in front of him.

"Yes?" she says.

"I'm sorry," he says.

She stands there, tapping her foot. Searching for words. She blurts them out as they come to her. "So, you got freaked out. I'm a lunatic. An X File. I figured it would happen."

"No—" he stands up.

"It's cool. No, really." She runs up the steps, past him, and fiddles for her key in the dark. "Now you know why I didn't want to tell anybody." The keys rattle in her fingers, and she cusses under her breath. "Least of all, you."

She drops the keys. "Goddamnit," she sniffs, picks them up again, and finds the right one.

"And if you tell anybody," her voice pitches higher as she gets the door open, "you'll learn a new definition of flagrant foul! You big . . . fucking . . . jerk!"

She slams the door.

11:22 p.m.

The phone rings.

"Asshole," she mutters. She picks it up.

"Will you let me explain?"

"No." She hangs up.

Waits.

Pours a glass of milk.

Drinks it.

Cusses.

Turns out the kitchen light, and goes to bed.

She is cursed for life. She will never have a boyfriend. Much less get married. Hell, she'll never be able to sleep with anybody.

She's a freak.
It's not fair.

Sobs shake the bed.

October 18, 2005, 7:39 a.m.

Janie calls the school, pretending to be her mother. "She won't be at school today. She has the flu."

She calls the nursing home. "I'm sick," she sniffles. "I can't come in tonight."

Everyone is sorry. The secretary. The nursing home director. "Feel better soon, sweetie," the director says.

But Janie knows there is no "better." This is it. This is her life.

She falls back in bed.

12:10 p.m.

Janie drags her ass out of bed and, sitting on her bedroom floor, does the homework she didn't do the previous night.

She can't stand getting behind in school.

She works ahead, even.

Her mother shuffles around the house, oblivious to Janie's presence. *The sleaze-bitch. It's her fault for giving birth to me*, she thinks. She'd blame her father, too, if she knew who he was. Briefly, she thinks of her mother's kaleidoscope dream. Wonders if the hippie Jesus is her father. Wonders what happened that made her mother give up on absolutely everything. She'll probably never know.

Maybe it's better this way.

2:55 p.m.

The phone rings. Janie's mother answers it.

"She's at school," she slurs.

Janie didn't know her mother ever answered the phone.

4:10 p.m.

Janie sits wrapped in a blanket on the couch, a roll of toilet paper next to her, watching *The Price Is Right*. Carrie lets herself in.

"Hey, bitch," she says cheerfully. "You missed a good one today. You sick?"

"Hey. Yeah." Janie blows her nose loudly in some toilet paper to prove it.

"You look like hell," Carrie says. "Your nose is all red."

"Thank you."

Carrie sits on the couch next to Janie.

"Funny . . . Cabel looks like hell too," she says lightly. "You sure you don't have something you want to tell me?"

"Pretty sure, yeah."

Carrie pouts. Then, she ruffles through her backpack and pulls out a folded piece of paper. She tosses it on the coffee table. "This is from him. You're not preggers or something, are you?"

Janie looks at Carrie. "Ha-ha."

"Well, jeez. Whatever it is, it's got to be a big deal to

keep you home from school. You haven't missed a day since eighth grade. And, sorry to say, you might look like shit, but I don't think you're sick."

"Think what you want," Janie says dully. "I think you have to have sex in order to get pregnant, last I heard."

"Aha, so it's a sex thing!" Carrie shouts triumphantly.

"Go home, Carrie."

Carrie grins. "You know where to find me. Sex tips and advice—just holler out the window."

Janie holds back an urge to strangle her. "Good-bye," she says pointedly.

"Okay, okay. I can take a hint." She heads to the door and turns back to Janie, a curious expression on her face. "This, by chance, doesn't have anything to do with Cabel messing with drugs this weekend, does it?" She blinks rapidly, grinning.

"What?"

"He's sort of a dealer, I guess—or, you know. One of those guys who works as a go-between. Whatever they're called. So Shay danced with him at a party Sunday night. She was really high, though. I heard he got busted. Is that true?"

Janie's stomach twists and shreds.

She's going to be sick.

"No," Janie says slowly, "it doesn't have anything to do

with that." Tears well up in the corners of her eyes and she presses them back with her fingers.

Carrie's face falls. "Oh, shit, Janie. You didn't know."

Janie shakes her head numbly.

She doesn't notice when Carrie leaves.

October 19, 2005, 2:45 a.m.

Janie lies awake in bed, staring at the ceiling. Arguing with herself. She knows she shouldn't do it. But she has nothing to lose.

Feeling like a total creep, she gets dressed and slips out of the house. Runs softly through the yards, avoiding the houses with dogs.

Sneaks up to Cabel's house and sits outside his bedroom window, in the bushes. She leans up against the house and waits. The bricks snag her sweatshirt. It's chilly. She puts her mittens on.

Her butt falls asleep.

And her legs.

She gets terribly bored.

5:01 a.m.

She slips away while it's still dark, feeling like a criminal.

A criminal who walks away with nothing.

7:36 a.m.

She gathers her schoolbooks from the coffee table. The note is still there, where Carrie left it. She hesitates, and then opens it.

We really need to talk, Janie. Please. I'm begging. Cabe.

That's all it says.

7:55 a.m.

Janie waits for the bell and slips into school. She gets to English class just before Mr. Purcell closes the door. "Feeling better, I presume, Miss Hannagan," he intones.

Janie *presumes* it's a rhetorical question and ignores him.

She can feel Cabel's eyes on her.

She won't look at him.

It's torture, is what it is.

Every damn class, of every damn day.

Torture.

12:45 p.m.

He gives up.

Janie dreads study hall. But he gives up. He sits in the opposite corner of the library, removes his glasses, and rests his head on his arms.

She notes with satisfaction that he does, indeed, look like shit. Just as Carrie said.

Carrie plops in the chair next to her.

If Cabel dreams, Janie doesn't pick it up. Instead, she lays her head on her arms and tries to take in a nap. But she's sucked into yet another falling dream. This time, it's her own.

And then she's pulled awake and Carrie is there. Or, rather, Janie is with Carrie. And Stu.

Janie watches with curiosity.

Carrie looks like she's enjoying it.

A lot.

Four times.

Once was enough for Janie.

And she really doesn't think Stu's dick could possibly be that large. He could have never fit behind the wheel of ol' Ethel with that thing.

Now Janie knows what else she's missing. She grunts when Carrie nudges her arm.

Gets up.

Two more classes.

Janie is weary. And she has to work a full shift tonight.

Apparently things get worse before they get better.

If they ever get better.

Janie's doubtful.

10:14 p.m.

Miss Stubin is in a coma.

Hospice is in her room all evening.

Janie hovers anxiously.

And then Miss Stubin dies. Right there in front of Janie.

Janie cries. She's not exactly sure why—she's never cried over a resident's death before. There was just something special about this one.

But she's glad Miss Stubin got to make love with that nice young soldier, even if it was just a black-and-white dream.

The head nurse sends Janie home a little early. She says Janie still looks a bit under the weather. Janie is numb. And exhausted. She's been awake since two a.m.

She says good-bye to Miss Stubin. Touches her cold, gnarled hand and gives it a little squeeze.

10:31 p.m.

Janie drives home slowly, windows rolled down, hand ready on the parking brake. She takes Waverly. Past Cabel's house.

Nothing.

She falls into bed when she gets home.

There are no notes, no phone calls, no visits. Not that she was hoping for anything, of course. That bastard.

October 22, 2005

Janie works the day shift. It's Saturday. She is assigned to the arts-and-crafts room. This makes her happy. Most of the residents at Heather Home don't sleep through the craft.

At her lunch break, the director is there, even though it's a weekend. She calls Janie into her office and closes the door.

Janie is worried. Has she done something wrong? Has someone caught her in a dream and thought she was slacking off? She sits down tentatively in the chair by the director's desk.

"Is everything okay?" she asks nervously.

The director smiles. She hands Janie an envelope. "This is for you," she says.

"What is it?"

"I don't know. It's something from Miss Stubin. We found it in her belongings after the coroner came. Open it."

Janie's eyes grow wide. Her fingers shake a little. She breaks open the seal and pulls out a folded piece of stationery. When she opens it, a small piece of paper flutters to the ground. She reads. The handwriting is barely legible. Crooked. Written with a blind hand.

Dear Janie,

Thank you for my dreams.

From one catcher to another,

Martha Stubin
P.S. You have more power than you think.

Janie's heart stutters. She draws in a breath. *No*, she thinks. Impossible.

The director picks up the small rectangle of paper from the floor and hands it to Janie. It's a check.

It says, "for college," in the memo line.

It's five thousand dollars.

Janie looks up at the director, whose face is beaming so hard, it looks like it's about to crack. She looks down at the check, and then again at the letter.

The director stands and gives Janie's shoulder a squeeze. "Good job, honey," she sniffles. "I'm so glad for you."

3:33 p.m.

There is a phone call for Janie.

She hurries to the front desk. What a strange day.

It's her mother.

"There's this hippie on the porch, says he ain't leaving until he talks to you. You coming home soon? He wants to know, and I'm going to bed."

Janie sighs. She writes her schedule down every week on the calendar. But she is amused. Maybe because she got a check from Miss Stubin. Maybe because her mother calls Cabel a hippie.

"I'll be home a little after five, Ma."

"Do I need to worry about this character on the porch, or can I go to bed?"

"You can go to bed. He's . . . ah . . . not a rapist." *That I know of, anyway.* They hang up.

5:21 p.m.

Cabel is not on the porch.

Janie goes inside. There's a note on the counter, underneath a dirty glass, in her mother's scrawl.

Hippie said he couldn't stay. Be back tomorrow.
Love, Mom.

It said, Love, Mom.

That was the most notable thing about it.

Janie rips the note into shreds and throws it in the overflowing garbage can.

She changes her clothes, pops a TV dinner in the oven, and pulls out her college applications.

Five thousand. Just a drop in the bucket, she knows. But it's something.

Just like Miss Stubin's note.

That was *really* something.

Janie can't wrap her mind around that one yet.

She looks over everything in her piles of papers. It all looks foreign to her. Financial aid forms, scholarship applications, writing a request essay? Jeez. She needs to get moving on this.

She has no idea what she wants to do with her future.

But science, math . . . maybe research. Maybe dream research.

Or not.

She really wants to forget that part of her shitty, shitty life.

She calls Carrie. "What're you doing?"

"Sitting home. Alone. You?"

"I'm wondering if there's a party somewhere at one of your rich friends' houses."

Carrie is silent for a moment. "Why?" Her voice is suspicious.

"I don't know," Janie lies. "I'm bored. Can't I get in with you? As your date or something?"

"Janie."

"What."

"You don't want to go there."

"What? I'm just bored. I've never been to one of those organized 'Hill' parties. You know, where the parents are gone and leave all the booze and shit for the kids to drink."

Carrie is quiet again. "You're looking for him, aren't you. I'm coming over." She hangs up.

Carrie arrives ten minutes later with her sleeping bag. "Can I stay over?" she asks sweetly. "We haven't had a sleepover in forever."

Janie looks at her skeptically. "What's going on?" she says. "Just tell me."

Carrie throws her stuff on the couch. "You got munchies? I haven't eaten." She sniffs the air and opens the oven. "Eww. Can't we cook something real?"

"Fine," sighs Janie. She rummages around in the kitchen. The refrigerator is surprisingly full today. "Fajitas okay?"

"Perfect," says Carrie gleefully. She mixes two vodka tonics, adds a splash of orange juice, and hands one to Janie.

"Would you stop that, please?"

"Stop what?"

"That whole syrupy sweet-talk thing. It's really grating on me."

Carrie blinks. "I don't know what you're talking about. Anyway, give me some friggin' veggies to chop."

They work up a meal, making guacamole from scratch and everything. Janie takes the TV dinner, wraps it in tinfoil, and puts it in the refrigerator. Her mother will probably eat it. Cold. For breakfast or something.

By the time the fajitas are ready, Janie is buzzing from her second drink and Carrie is doing shots from the bottle.

They move into the living room and flip on music videos.

"So, are you going to tell me what the fuck is going on, or not," Janie says.

Carrie sighs and gives her a sorrowful look. "Oh, Janie. Are you still thumpin' for Cabel or what?"

Janie takes a swallow of her drink, and lies. "I . . . I'm getting over him. I'm not speaking to him."

"I saw him here, on your step this morning. Were you working?"

"Yeah. I guess he was here all day. Ma calls him 'the hippie.'" She laughs.

Carrie takes another shot. "Whooo!" she says when it goes down. "Sheesh. Um . . . oh, yeah. Cabel. Well, he's at Melinda's tonight. With Shay," she adds.

"Well, duh, he wouldn't be with Melinda."

Carrie gives her a curious look. "Why not Melinda?"

Janie's feeling a bit reckless from the effects of the alcohol. "Carrie! Melinda's a lesbian. Didn't you know?"

"What?"

"She's totally in love with you."

"She is not."

"Is."

"How do you know?"

Janie hesitates.

She knows she shouldn't say it.

But she does. "She dreams about you. I've seen her dreams."

Carrie looks at her, confused.

Janie sits, stone-faced.

And then Carrie bursts out laughing. "Holy shit, Janes. You got your funny back."

Janie echoes Carrie's laugh. "Gotcha," she says shakily.

Carrie takes a tentative bite of her fajita. "Hey, it's good, kiddo."

Janie rolls her eyes. Now Stu has Carrie calling her that. "Anyway," prompts Janie.

"Hunh?"

"Cabel?"

"Ohhhh. Right. Well, since you dumped him, he's been going whole hog on the rich girls. He's got Shay wrapped around his little finger."

"Even though he supposedly got busted at her party?"

Carrie giggles. "Who do you think he's working with? Her father! They have a little 'arrangement.' Shay told me. How hilarious is that. Talk about a family business. And we're not talking just pot."

Janie shovels food in her mouth.

Carrie continues. "Shay told Melinda she slept with him." She slaps her hand to her mouth. "Oh, my God. I did not just say that."

Janie is numb. And strangely begging for more. She wants to hate him. "Naw, it's cool," she says smoothly. "I'm so over that guy. He's a big fake. Right?" She eggs Carrie on.

"He IS a big fake," shrieks Carrie, nearly upsetting the vodka bottle. She fills Janie's glass. "No wonder he has all those new clothes, and finally got a cell phone. Sheesh. He's making some bucks. I think it's crack. But that's just a guess."

Janie can't believe it.

He said he doesn't drink. Doesn't do drugs.

She thought he couldn't stand Shay Wilder.

What a liar.

"All the dealers lie, I suppose," Janie says.

Carrie nods, overanimated by the liquor. "They are pretty smooth. I just couldn't believe it when I found out what Cabel was doing. But I knew he was a pothead three years ago, back after he flunked into our grade. I guess it goes on from there."

"Was he really a pothead then?"

"I bought from him," Carrie whispers.

"You did?"

Carrie nods again. "A lot."

Janie stands abruptly and takes the dishes to the sink. She begins washing them as the flurry of information sloshes around in her brain. He had sex with Shay? Janie's whole body stings.

When Janie comes back to the living room, Carrie's eyes are glazed. She stares at the TV.

Janie sits next to her. "So if Cabel is hot for Shay, why did he sit on my step all day, and why does he keep trying to talk to me?"

Carrie looks at Janie. "Maybe he doesn't want to lose you as a future customer. Or a good lay. Face it, baby, you're looking hot these days."

Janie feels her stomach churning.

She excuses herself to the bathroom.

When she returns, Carrie's lying on the couch, passed out.

Janie turns off the TV. She cleans up the mess and gets a drink of water.

October 23, 2005 1:34 a.m.

She leaves Carrie on the couch, sprints through the yards to hide in the stand of trees near Cabel's house. There's a light on inside, so she waits. After a while, a car pulls into his driveway. It sits there for five minutes, maybe more. Finally, Cabel gets out and goes inside. When she sees all the lights go out, she deposits herself in the bushes under his window, stepping carefully around the crunchy leaves that insist on falling constantly the past few days.

Luck is on her side when he cracks the window open an inch. She hears him now, and her heart breaks as he sighs and rustles around in the dark. She can hear his bed creak when he lies down, and she can hear him punch his pillow, getting settled for sleep.

She wonders what he wears to bed. She is more than tempted to look.

But she will wait.

She must wait.

She waits.

2:15 a.m.

He doesn't snore.

3:04 a.m.

Janie, asleep in the bushes, is jolted awake. Painfully.

Her body is paralyzed almost immediately, and she is sucked into his mind. Into his fears. His dream.

It lasts two hours.

The same scenes, on an endless loop.

The middle-aged man, spraying lighter fluid, and then flicking a cigarette at Cabel. The monster-man in the kitchen, flinging a knife-pointed chair, hitting the ceiling fan, decapitating the middle-aged man. And a new one. Shay, the rich girl cheerleader, in handcuffs, hooked to a bed. Smiling.

Janie thinks she looks dreadful.

Naked.

As Cabel climbs in bed with her.

And Janie can't pull herself away.

She feels herself become ill, but she cannot move.

She can't pound on the window to wake him.

She's frozen. Paralyzed.

And she thought school was torture.

It's absolutely the worst dream she's ever been stuck in. By far. She passes out. Unconscious. Drained. Right before the scene changes. And ends.

6:31 a.m.

She opens her eyes.

On her belly, facedown, in the stones and branches.

She can hardly move.

But she must.

The sun is coming up.

7:11 a.m.

Janie limps home. Ignores the barking dogs.

7:34 a.m.

Janie crawls in the door, closes it, and falls on the carpet next to Carrie, who is still lying on the couch. She sleeps.

8:03 a.m.

Oh, God. She's in the forest. Again, again, again. So tired.

When they see the boy, bobbing in the water, Stu appears next to Carrie.

The grin.

The struggling.

The plea. Help him.

And Janie can't help him.

She can never help him.

Stu reaches over the water, but he cannot help either. Stu makes love to Carrie as she is crying for the boy, Carson.

The boy is bloody, lost, gone with the shark.

As always.

Janie cries. For Carson, for Carrie. But mostly for herself. She feels like she's about a hundred years old.

9:16 a.m.

Carrie nudges Janie.

"I gotta go," she says.

Janie grunts. Her body aches.

Carrie closes the door softly, and Janie sleeps.

The carpet scratches her face.

11:03 a.m.

There is a soft knock, and a lets-himself-in noise of the door. Janie thinks she's dreaming.

He checks to make sure she is alive, on the floor. Then he sits on the couch and waits.

Janie's mother walks by.

And walks by again, the other way, carrying a tinfoil-covered tray and a glass bottle.

12:20 p.m.

She rolls.

Groans.

Curls up in a ball on her side, clutching her belly.

"Oh, God," she moans, eyes closed. Her head aches. Her muscles scream every time she moves. She is weak and empty. Light-headed. Exhausted.

And he is there, picking her up. Taking her to her bed. Covering her with blankets.

He closes the door.

Sits on the floor, next to her.

12:54 p.m.

He goes to the kitchen. Makes her a cold chicken sandwich. Pours milk. Pours orange juice. Puts it on a plate. Takes it to her room.

Waits.

1:02 p.m.

Until he gets scared because she's sleeping so much. And he wakes her up.

Janie groans and slowly sits up.

She drinks the juice and milk.

Eats the sandwich.

Doesn't look at Cabel.

Or speak to him.

1:27 p.m.

"Why do you keep coming here," she says dully. Her voice is rough.

He measures his words. "Because I care about you."

She chuckles morosely. "Right."

He looks at her helplessly. "Janie, I'm—"

She gives him a sharp look. "You're what? Dealing drugs? Fucking Shay Wilder? Tell me something I don't know."

He puts his head in his hands and groans. "Don't believe everything you hear."

She snorts. "You're denying it?"

"I am not fucking Shay Wilder." He shudders.

"Oh, really. Only in your dreams, then." She turns to the wall.

He stares at the back of her head.

For a painful amount of time.

"You didn't," he finally says.

She doesn't respond.

He stands up. "Jesus, Janie." He spits the words.

Stands there, accusing.

"Maybe you should leave now," Janie says.

He moves to the door, opens it, and turns back to look at her. "Dreams are not memories, Janie. They're hopes and fears. Indications of other life stresses. I thought you of all people would know the difference." He walks out.

November 21, 2005

Janie and Cabel don't speak.

Janie goes about school and her job mechanically, feeling emptier than she's ever felt before in all her life. The one person who knows about the dreams, the one person she really started to care about, feels like her worst enemy. Janie spends a lot of time thinking about being an old maid forever, like Miss Stubin. Preparing herself for a very lonely life.

Working at the nursing home.

Commuting to college.

Living with her mother.

Forever.

At school, the number of sleeping students increases with the waning of daylight hours and the onset of colder weather.

As Thanksgiving approaches, in one especially rough study hall that follows too light a lunch, a science geek girl named Stacey O'Grady takes a rare nap. She's driving an out-of-control car with a rapist in the backseat for almost the entire class period. Fifteen minutes into it, Janie is already fully paralyzed.

Luckily, Carrie is not there to notice when Janie falls off her chair and shakes on the carpet, back in the corner of the library.

Luckily, Cabel notices.

He picks her up, sets her back on the chair.

Rubs her fingers a bit until they move.

Pulls a king-size Snickers bar from his backpack and sets it next to her hand before he leaves for government class.

Distracts the teacher when she slips in late.

Doesn't look at her.

Janie swallows her pride along with the candy bar. Writes something in her spiral notebook in a shaky hand. Rips the paper off the spiral.

Crumbles it into a ball.

Hits him in the back of the head with it.

He picks it up and opens it. Reads it.

Smiles, and puts it in his backpack.

On Ethel's windshield after school is a section of newspaper—the classifieds. Janie looks around suspiciously, wondering if it's some sort of joke. Seeing no one, she pulls it out from under the wiper and gets in the car. She gives it a cursory glance, first one side, and then the other. And then she finds it. Highlighted in yellow.

Having trouble sleeping? Nightmares? Sleep disorders?
Questions answered. Problems solved.

It's a volunteer sleep study. Sponsored by the University of Michigan. For scientific research.

And it's free.

When she gets home, she calls immediately and signs up for Thanksgiving weekend, at the North Fieldridge Sleep Clinic location near school.

November 25, 2005

It's the day after Thanksgiving. Janie worked Thanksgiving Day and today, for double pay. She has tomorrow off, anticipating trouble at the sleep study tonight. Wondering if this is going to be a repeat of the bus ride to Stratford. Wondering if this is going to turn into another big mess.

10:59 p.m.

She grabs an overnight bag from the backseat of her car and walks into the sleep clinic. She removes her coat and registers under a fake name at the desk. Through the tinted glass window, she can see a row of beds with machines all around. There are people already in some of the beds.

This is a very, very bad idea, she thinks.

The door to the sleep room opens, and a woman in a white lab coat stands there, looking at a chart. Janie stumbles. Puts her hands to her face. Grimaces. She reaches blindly for a chair before her body goes numb.

11:01 p.m.

She is on a street in a busy city. It's raining. She stands under an awning, not sure who she's looking for. Not yet. She doesn't feel compelled to follow anyone passing by. Eventually, her stomach lurches. She sighs and rolls her eyes, and looks up.

Here he comes, she thinks.

Through the awning.

It's Mr. Abernethy, the principal of her high school.

11:02 p.m.

Her vision defrosts. The lab-coated woman has moved into the room and is staring at her.

Janie stares back, just to freak her out. She looks around the room at the others who sit there, waiting for their names to be called. They all look at the floor as her gaze passes from one to the next. She knows what they're thinking. *There's no way they want to be in that room with me, the freak.*

Janie sets her jaw.

She's tired of crying.

Refuses to make any further scenes.

When the feeling returns to her fingers and feet, she stands up, grabs her coat and overnight bag, and stumbles to the door.

Her voice is hoarse when she turns to speak to the receptionist. "Sorry. I'm not doing this." She goes outside into the parking lot. The air is crisp, and she sucks it into her lungs.

The woman in the lab coat chases out the door after her. "Miss?"

Janie keeps walking. Tosses her bag back into the car.

Over her shoulder, she yells, "I said, I'm not doing this."

She climbs behind the wheel. Leaves the lab-coated woman standing there as she drives away. "There has to be another way, Ethel," she says. "You understand me, don't you sweetheart."

Ethel purrs mournfully.

11:23 p.m.

Janie pulls into her driveway after the incident in the sleep study waiting room. Wonders if she should have given it a try. But there is no way on earth she wants to know what her principal, Mr. Abernethy, dreams about.

Ew.

Ew, ew, ew.

This is not the right way to fix it, she decides. But what is the right way? Because it's time.

Time to stop crying, time to get her act together and do something. Time to move beyond the pity party.

Before she loses her mind.

Because there's no way on earth she's going to make it through college unless she grows some serious ovaries and turns this train wreck around.

She goes into the house and digs through her papers on her bedside table. She finds it—Miss Stubin's note. Reads it again.

Dear Janie,

Thank you for my dreams.

From one catcher to another,

Martha Stubin

P.S. You have more power than you think.

11:36 p.m.

What does it mean?

11:39 p.m.

She still doesn't know.

11:58 p.m.

Nope.

November 26, 2005, 9:59 a.m.

Janie waits at the door of the public library. When it opens for business, she meanders through the nonfiction section. Self-help. Dreams.

She pulls all six books from the shelf, finds a back corner table, and reads.

When a group of sleepy-looking students comes in and sets up at a nearby table, she moves to a different section of the library.

And she waits patiently for the computer in the corner to open up. Spends an hour there. She can't believe what she finds with Google's help.

Of course, there's no information on people like her. But it's a start.

5:01 p.m.

With four of the six books in tow, Janie drives home. She is fascinated. She makes dinner with a book in her hand. She reads until midnight. And then she takes a deep breath and talks to herself as she gets ready for bed.

"I have a problem," she says quietly, trying not to feel like a dork. "I have a problem, and I need to solve it. I would like to have a dream about how to solve this problem."

She concentrates. Climbs into bed, closes her eyes, and continues in a calm voice. "I would like to dream about what I can do to block out other people's dreams. I want—" she falters. "I mean, I would like to help people, and I also . . . would like . . . to live a normal life. So their dreams don't fuck up my life forever."

Janie breathes deeply. She stops speaking, and instead focuses her mind on her problem. Until she remembers. "And I would like to remember the dream when I wake up," she adds out loud.

Over and over, she repeats the words in her head.

She peeks at the clock quickly and chides herself for messing with the mojo.

12:33 a.m.

She focuses again. Breathes deeply. Lets the thoughts float around and meld together in her mind.

Slowly, she feels the thoughts filling the room. She breathes them in. They caress her skin. She lets her mind be free, allows her muscles to relax.

And she lets the sleep in.

Nothing happens at first.

Which is good, she discovers.

Lucidity comes late.

2:45 a.m.

Janie finds herself in the middle of a dark lake. She treads water for what seems like hours. She grows weary. Panics. Sees Cabel on the shore with a rope. She waves frantically to him, but he doesn't see her. She can't hold on. The water fills her mouth and ears.

She submerges.

There are many people under the surface of the water—men, women, children, babies. She looks at them with panic, her lungs bursting. They stare at her, eyes bulging in death.

She looks around frantically. The pressure in her lungs is overpowering. Everything dims, and goes black. She feels her eyeballs bulging, and hears the haunting inner laughter of the floating bodies around her.

Janie gasps and sits up. It's 3:10 a.m.

She breathes hard. Writes down the dream in a spiral notebook.

Tries not to feel bad that she failed. She expects this.

It's not over, she tells herself, lying back down.

Let me dream it again, she thinks, calmly. *And this time, I won't drown. I will breathe under water, because this is my dream and I can do what I want with it. I will swim like a fish. Because I know how to swim. And . . . and I have gills. Yes, that's it. I have gills.*

She repeats this to herself as she lies down.

3:47 a.m.

She doesn't have gills.

She rolls over and groans, frustrated, into her pillow. Repeats the mantra.

4:55 a.m.

It begins again.

When Janie slips under water, exhausted, her lungs burning, she looks around at the others who are floating under the surface.

She begins to panic.

The bulging eyes.

And then.

Miss Stubin blinks at her from under the water. She smiles encouragingly. She is not one of the dead.

Floating next to Miss Stubin is another Janie, who nods and smiles. "It's your dream," she says.

The drowning Janie looks from Miss Stubin to Janie. Her vision dims.

She grows frantic.

"Concentrate," Janie says. "Change it."

Drowning Janie closes her eyes. Falls farther under the water. She kicks her feet as she loses consciousness, struggling to move, to get back above the water.

"Concentrate!" Janie says again. "Do it!"

Gills pop from the drowning Janie's neck.

She opens her eyes.

Breathes. Long, cleansing breaths, underwater. It tickles. She laughs in bubbles, incredulous.

She looks up, and Miss Stubin and Janie are smiling. Clapping, slow motion and soundless, in the water. They swim over to her.

The formerly drowning Janie grins. "I did it," she says. Bubbles come out of her mouth, and the words appear individually above her head when each bubble pops, like a cartoon.

"You did it," Janie says, nodding, her hair swishing like silk.

"Let's swim now," Miss Stubin says. "Someone's waiting for you on the shore."

Janie and Miss Stubin swim partway with the formerly drowning Janie, and then they stop and wave her on.

She nears the shore, and when she surfaces and can stand, the gills disappear. She walks out of the water, streaming wet in her pajamas—boxer shorts and a T-shirt.

Cabel is there. He's wearing boxer shorts too. His muscles ripple in the sunlight. His body is tan. It glistens.

It looks like they are on a deserted, tropical island.

He doesn't move.

He doesn't have a rope anymore.

He's sitting in the sand.

She waits for him to do something, but he doesn't move.

"Remember, it's your dream," she hears. It's her other Janie speaking, the one who is aware that she is dreaming.

Janie hesitates and approaches Cabel. "Hey, Cabel."

He looks up. "I care about you," he says. His eyes are brown and turning muddy.

Janie wants to believe him. And so she does.

"What about Shay?" she asks.

"Dreams aren't memories," he says. "Please talk to me."

6:29 a.m.

Janie smiles in her sleep. She watches over herself in the dream, and plunges back into it, taking it in different directions, starting over at various spots to make it fun, or sexy, or beautiful, or silly.

November 27, 2005, 8:05 a.m.

The alarm clock rings. Janie keeps her eyes closed and reaches to turn it off. She lies in bed, going over the dream in detail, remembering it. Memorizing it.

When she has it solidly in her mind, she sits up and writes it in her journal.

She can't stop smiling.

It's a small step. But it gives Janie hope.

She studies the books all day, until it's time for work.

9:58 p.m.

It's quiet at the nursing home. The residents are all tucked in their beds, doors closed. Janie fills out charts at the front desk. She is alone.

The call panel is dark, until a white light flashes from the room Miss Stubin once occupied. A new resident is there now. His name is Johnny McVicker.

Janie sets down her pen and goes into the room to see what he needs.

But Mr. McVicker is asleep.

He's dreaming.

Janie grabs hold of the wall as she goes blind.

9:59 p.m.

They are in the basement of a house. It's lit moderately, and it's not very cold down there. Janie sees gray leaves blowing and piling up outside the venting window. Everything is in black and white, she realizes after a moment.

Mr. McVicker is perhaps twenty years younger. He stands at the bottom of the stairs with a young man, whom he calls Edward.

They are yelling.

Hateful things.

Mr. McVicker looks horrified, and Edward storms up the stairs and out of the house, slamming the door.

The old man tries to follow, but he can only move in slow motion. He tries speaking, but no words come out. He is mired by the weight of his feet, sinking through the steps.

He looks at Janie, his face cracked and broken, lined with tears. And then he looks past Janie.

Janie turns around.

Miss Stubin is standing behind her, watching. Waiting. For something. She smiles encouragingly at Mr. McVicker.

His face is anguished.

Fresh tears fall from his eyes.

He is sinking into the steps, and now he can't move at all.

Miss Stubin stands patiently, watching him, compassionate. She closes her eyes, and her brow furrows. She holds deathly still.

"Help me," he finally cries, as if it's forced from his lungs.

Miss Stubin glides over to Mr. McVicker.

Holds her hand out.

Helps him out of the stairs, which magically repair themselves. But instead of guiding him up the stairs, she brings him back to the starting spot of the dream.

Miss Stubin glances at Janie and nods, then turns back to the old man and tells him something that Janie cannot hear.

They stand there, Janie looking on, for several moments. And then the dream begins again.

Mr. McVicker and Edward are yelling.

Hateful things.

Mr. McVicker looks horrified, and Edward turns toward the stairs.

Miss Stubin says something to Mr. McVicker again. The scene pauses.

Mr. McVicker reaches for Edward's sleeve.

"Don't go," he says. "Please. There's something I have to tell you."

Edward turns around slowly.

"Son," the old man says. "You're right. I'm wrong. And I'm so sorry."

Edward's lip quivers.

He opens his arms to his father.

Mr. McVicker embraces the young man. "I love you," he says.

Miss Stubin whispers a third time to Mr. McVicker, and he nods and smiles. He puts his arm around his son, and they walk up the stairs together.

Miss Stubin smiles at Janie and fades away. Janie stands for a moment in the basement. She is surprised that she's not compelled to follow the old man. She looks around and sees bright green grass and petunias growing outside the venting window, and the basement walls have turned a soft yellow.

Strange.

Janie closes her eyes and concentrates, and she pulls herself easily from the dream.

She's still standing. She blinks Mr. McVicker's dark room into view once again. Her fingers are barely tingling.

How bizarre.

But nice to see Miss Stubin. That's for sure.

She turns to leave. Out of the corner of her eye, she notices his call button.

It's on the floor.

Out of reach of the bed.

Janie hesitates, and then picks it up and connects it back to its clip on the wall. She turns the blinking light off.

She looks around the room quickly, hackles raised.

Closes the door behind her.

Shakes her head, mystified.

At the front desk is Carol, the head nurse. "I finished your charts, hon," she says. "Where'd you disappear off to?"

Janie points down the hall. "Mr. McVicker's light was flashing. He's all set now. I just turned it off." Her voice is pure and smooth, and it catches her by surprise.

Carol gives her a curious look. "His light wasn't flashing, Janie." She goes to the light panel, picks it up, and jiggles it. "Hmm," she says. "Maybe it burned out."

"That's odd," Janie says lightly.

She puts the charts away, grabs her coat, and punches out. The stamp says 11:09 p.m. "Welp, gotta go. School tomorrow."

She drives home, a fresh song in her heart.

November 29, 2005, 12:45 p.m.

Janie is obsessed with learning more about dreams. She wills people to sleep in class. And study hall, as always, is full of excitement.

Janie practices on everyone she can.

Most of the time, she fails.

She still hasn't figured everything out.

But she will.

By God, she will.

Because now she has her very good friend Miss Stubin to help her. She suppresses the urge to skip down the hallways.

December 5, 2005, 7:35 a.m.

Cabel parks his new car next to Janie's as she arrives at school.

It's not a brand-new car. Just new to him.

But it *is* a Beemer.

People on the south side of Fieldridge do not drive Beemers. Well, maybe the 1976 variety. Definitely not the 2000 variety. Janie's mouth opens, and then she presses her lips shut. Shakes her head and walks toward the building.

He's right behind her. "It's six years old, Janie. Come on."

Janie's eyebrow is permanently raised as he tries to keep up with her on the way in to school.

She loses him when he slips and flips on the icy sidewalk.

Janie finds Carrie by the doorway to English class. "What's the scoop on the pimpster wheels out there?" Janie asks her.

"I don't know, *chica*. He must be makin' some big cake. I can't believe he hasn't been expelled yet."

"Has he actually been arrested?"

"No. Shay's daddy worked it out with the cops. Cabel was at all the parties this weekend with her."

"And now he's driving that."

"It's a friggin' 323Ci convertible. Stu says seventeen grand at least for one of those, used."

Janie's blood boils. "This is just . . . just . . ." The anger swells, and she can't come up with a word. Carrie is giving her the evil eye.

"Unbefuckinglievable?" comes a voice from behind her.

She takes a quick breath, watching Carrie's eyes grow wide. "Shit." She turns around and there's Cabel.

"S'cuse me, please," he says politely, and squeezes past them into the classroom. Janie catches a whiff of the cologne he's wearing. Her stomach flips against her will.

Carrie's eyes sparkle. She giggles. "Oops."

Janie rolls her eyes and laughs reluctantly. "Yeah."

12:45 p.m.

For days, Janie's been in other people's dreams during study hall, with minimal success in helping them change the dreams. She is still puzzled by one thing.

Make that two things.

First, how did Miss Stubin get Mr. McVicker to ask her for help? And second, what was she saying to him to get him to change his dream?

Sorry. Make that three. Three things.

How the hell can Miss Stubin see in the dreams, when she's blind? And how can she be there when she's dead?

Okay, that's four. Janie knows. There are probably more than that, even.

This is so frustrating.

She knows she needs to work harder.

And she's losing weight. Rapidly.

She was already thin enough.

Now her cheeks look caved in, like her mother's. And she has dark circles under her eyes, from getting up so often in the night, working on her own dreams.

She finds Snickers bars in the strangest places.

(She knows they're from him.)

(She wonders if they're laced with pot.)

Cabel has been sitting in his old spot again the past few weeks. But he doesn't sleep.

He reads.

Janie sort of wishes he would fall asleep. But she also worries what she might see.

Exams are coming. She opens her math book and studies it. Every now and then, she glances at Cabel, whose back is to her. From what Carrie said, he was at the Hill parties again all weekend. With Shay. And a lot of drugs. Janie sighs. Pulls herself out of the threatening misery and focuses on the math book again. Refuses to go there.

1:01 p.m.

Cabel's head nods, and jerks back up. He shakes his head swiftly and glances over his shoulder at Janie. Janie looks down. Then he slouches in his chair and puts his chin in his hand. His hair falls softly around his shoulders and over his eyes. Janie reluctantly admires his profile as he turns a page in the book.

His head nods.

The book slips from his fingers.

It doesn't wake him when it thumps on the table.

Janie feels his energy.

She concentrates, and slips into his dream slowly. Another positive step—she's learning to control the speed of her arrivals and departures. It's much easier than —

1:03 p.m.

He's sitting in a dark jail cell. Alone. Above his head is a sign that says, "Drug Pusher."

Janie watches from outside the cell.

His head is down.

The scene changes abruptly.

He's in Janie's room, sitting on the floor, writing something on a pad of paper. Alone. He looks up at her, beckoning her with his eyes. She takes a few steps forward.

He holds up the notepad.

It's not what you think.

That's what it says.

He tears off that sheet of paper. Below it is another sheet in his handwriting.

I think I'm in love with you.

Janie's stomach lurches.

He looks at the tablet for a long moment. Then he turns to Janie and rips off one more sheet. He watches her face as she reads it.

How do you like my new trick?

He grins at her, and fades.

The scene changes again. Back in the jail cell. The sign above his head is gone.

He is alone. She watches from outside. His head is down. Then he looks up at her.

A ring of keys floats in front of her.

"Let me out," he says. "Help me."

Janie is startled. She moves automatically and unlocks the cell. He walks to her, takes her in his arms. He looks into her eyes. He sinks his fingers into her hair and kisses her.

Janie steps out of herself as she's kissing Cabel. She walks away into a dark hallway and eases herself back to awareness in the library.

She blinks.

Sits up.

Looks at him.

He's still asleep at his table.

She rubs her eyes and wonders:

How the hell did he do that?

And.

Now what?

1:30 p.m.

He slides into the seat across the table from Janie. His eyes are moist with sleep and mischief. "Well?"

"Well what," she mutters.

"It worked, right?"

Janie squelches a grin. Poorly. "How the hell did you do that?" she demands.

His face sobers. "It's the only way I could think of to get you to talk to me."

"Okay, I get that. But how did you do it?"

He hesitates. Glances at the clock. Shrugs. "Doesn't

look like I have time to explain right now," he says. "When would you like to go out with me so we can talk about it?" A grin flirts with his lips.

He's got her cornered.

And he knows it.

Janie chuckles, defeated. "You are such a bastard."

"When," he demands. "I promise, all my heart, I'll be your house elf for the rest of my life if I fail to meet you at the appointed date and time." He leans forward. "Promise," he says again. He holds up two fingers.

The bell rings.

They stand up.

She's not answering.

He comes around the table toward her and pushes her gently against the wall. Sinks his lips into hers.

He tastes like spearmint.

She can't stop the flipping in her stomach.

He pulls back and touches her cheek, her hair. "When," he whispers. Urgently.

She clears her throat and blinks. "A-a-after school works for me," she says.

They grab their backpacks and run. As they slip in the doorway of government class, he shoves a PowerBar in her hand.

She sits at her desk and looks at it. She raises her

eyebrow at him, from across the room.

"Protein," he mouths. He gestures like a weight lifter.

She laughs out loud.

Opens it.

Sneaks bites when the teacher isn't looking.

It's not as good as a Snickers.

But it'll do.

In P.E., they're playing badminton.

"I'm watching you," he growls as they change sides. "Don't you dare sneak out of here without me."

She flashes him a wicked grin.

After school, Janie exits the locker room and looks around, then heads for the parking lot. He's standing between their cars. His hair, dripping, has a few tiny icicles attached.

"Aha!" he says when he sees her, as if he's foiled her escape plans.

She rolls her eyes. "Where to, dreamboy?"

Cabel hesitates.

Works his jaw.

"My house," he says. "You lead the way."

She freezes. Her stomach churns. "Is . . . is he . . ." She swallows hard.

He squints in the pale sunlight and reads the question in her voice. "Don't worry, Janie. He's dead."

WHAT BECOMES THE LONGEST DAY

It's still December 5, 2005

Three o'clock.

Janie pulls into Cabel's driveway, tentatively. He pulls in behind her and jumps out of the car, grabbing his backpack and closing his car door gently. It clicks perfectly, solid. "I just love that sound," he says wistfully. "Anyway. Follow me."

He opens the rickety service door to the garage. It creaks and groans. He flips on the garage light and takes Janie by the hand. The garage is tidy. It smells pleasant, like old grass clippings and gasoline. Next to the door that leads into the house hangs Cabel's skateboard. Janie smiles and touches it.

"Remember that?" she says. "That was a sweet thing

for you to do. I hadn't exactly planned on walking home that night."

"How could I forget. You slammed the gymnasium door handle right into my gut."

"That was you?"

He gives her a patronizing smile. "Indeed."

They go inside.

The house is tiny. Clean. Threadbare.

She startles when she sees the kitchen. She's seen this room before, in his dream. The table. And the chairs.

"Jesus," she says under her breath. She looks up. The ceiling fan is there. "Oh, God." She turns and looks where the front door would be, where the middle-aged man came in, and it beckons to her. She drops her backpack on the floor, shuts her eyes, and covers her face with her hands.

And he's touching her shoulders.

Wrapping his arms around her.

Stroking her hair.

Whispering, his lips to her ear. "He's not here. It's just a dream. That never happened. Never happened." And she's soothed by the words. She breathes him in. Her hands leave her face and find his shoulders, his chest. She touches his chest lightly, wondering if scars lie beneath his shirt. Wonders if *that* dream really happened. And then he's kissing her neck and she's falling, turning her head to find his mouth with her lips, and she's tracing his jaw with her fingertips and kissing him hard, their tongues tasting each other madly, and he's pressing into her and she into him, bodies shivering, like they are two scared, lost children, starving, starving to be touched, to be held, by someone, anyone, the first one they can find who seems familiar enough, safe enough, strong enough to rescue them. They breathe, heavy. Hard. Their fingers strain at cotton.

And then they slow down.

Stop. Hold. Rest.

Before one of them, or both, begins to sob.

Before they break another piece that needs to be fixed.

They stand together for a moment, collecting.

And then he finds her fingers and strings them in his, and leads her to the living room.

On the coffee table rests a stack of books.

He looks at Janie. "This is how," he says, his voice catching. "You know these books now, don't you."

"Yes," she says. She kneels next to the table and lays the dream books out.

"I've been practicing," he says. "Hoping."

Dreaming, she adds silently. "Tell me."

He sits beside her with two sodas and an apology. "I don't have anything stronger," he says. "Anyway. I read this book about lucid dreams and taught myself to dream what I wanted to dream about."

She smiles. "Yup. I did it too."

"Good." He sounds businesslike. "What about the sleep clinic?"

"Ugh. Great idea, but not cool, as it turned out. I went in, got stuck in a dream when the lab tech opened the door to the sleep room. Walked out." She pauses. "It was Mr. Abernethy's dream. I just didn't want to know what that country-fried rube was dreaming about."

Cabel chokes on his Pepsi. "Good call." He grows serious a moment, thinking. But then waves the thought away. "Yeah. Really good call."

"Huh?"

"Nothing. Okay, so I first tried to dream me saying specific things to you. But I couldn't get it to happen right. Too much"—he pauses, glancing sidelong at her—"too much came out of my mouth. More than I wanted to say. I couldn't control it." He shifts in his seat. "So I thought I was screwed. But then I thought of writing the words on the page. I practiced it a bunch of times, and the last few nights it worked."

"But you didn't dream me into the dream. At least, not until the end."

"Right. Because I could control it better if I had myself alone, knowing that if—when—I dreamed it around you, you would be there."

Janie closes her eyes, picturing it. "Clever," she murmurs. She opens her eyes. "Really clever, Cabe."

"So you could read the tablet?" he says. His face flushes a little.

"Yes."

"All of it?"

She searches his face. "Yes."

"And?"

She's quiet. "I don't know what to say. I'm really confused."

He takes her hand and leans back on the couch. "I have a lot of explaining to do. Will you hear me out?"

She takes a breath, and lets it out slowly. All the reasons to hate him flood back into her brain. Her self-protective nature percolates. She does not want to ride this roller coaster again. "Well," she says finally, "I can't imagine I'll believe a word of it. You've been lying to me from the beginning, Cabe. Since before, well, anything." Her voice catches.

She looks away.

Withdraws her hand from his.

Stands up abruptly. "Bathroom?" she squeaks.

"Fuck," he mutters. "Through the kitchen, first door on the right."

She finds it, sobs silently over the sink for a moment, blows her nose, and sits on the edge of the tub until she gets it together again. Realizes she's already on this roller coaster, and sitting in the front car.

When she gets to the living room, he's ending a cell-phone call, saying "tomorrow" firmly, elbows on his knees and his head in his hands. He flips the phone off.

"Look," he says in a dull voice, not looking at her. "There's some shit I can't tell you. Not yet. Maybe not for a while. But I'll answer any question—any question I can right now. If I can't, and you don't like that, you are free to hate me forever. I won't bother you."

She is confused. "Okay," she says slowly. Decides to start with an easy one. "Who were you talking to, just now."

He closes his eyes. Groans. "Shay."

Janie stands in the doorway to the living room, tottering. Furious tears spring to her eyes. But when she speaks, her voice is deadly calm. "Jesus Christ, Cabe." She turns and grabs her backpack and walks firmly out the same way they entered the house.

Gets in her car.

She can't get out of the driveway.

She thinks about ramming his pimpmobile.

But that wouldn't be nice for Ethel.

"Goddamnit!" she screams, and puts her head on the steering wheel. She can't even drive through the yard without hurting Ethel, because of the stupid drainage ditch.

And then she hears the front door slam. He's running to move his car. He starts it up and pulls it into the grass next to hers so she can back out.

She doesn't know why she's waiting.

He's coming to her window.

She can still go now.

He taps.

She hesitates, and then rolls down the window an inch.

"I'm so sorry, Janie," he says.

He's bawling.

He goes back inside.

She sits in the driveway, freezing, for thirty-six minutes. Arguing with herself.

Because she thinks she's in love with him too. And there are two ways she can be a fool in love right now.

She chooses the harder one.

And knocks on the door.

He's on the phone again when he opens it. His eyes are rimmed in red. "I'll try," he says, and hangs up the phone. Stands there. Looking like shit.

"Let's try this again," Janie says, angry, hands on her hips. "Who were you talking to on the phone just now, Cabe?" Her words slice through the crisp air.

"My boss."

She's taken aback for a moment. "You mean your dealer? Your pimp?" The sarcasm rings in the dusky house.

He closes his eyes. "No."

She stands there. Uncertain.

He opens his eyes. Takes off his glasses and wipes his face with his sleeve. His voice has lost all hope. "Is there any chance," he says evenly, "that you'll come for a ride with me? My boss is interested in talking to you."

She blinks. She gets nervous. "Why?" she asks.

"I can't tell you. You'll have to trust me."

Janie takes a step back. The words ring familiar in her ears. She asked the same of him once.

She deliberates.

"I'll drive separately," she says quietly.

4:45 p.m.

She follows his car to downtown Fieldridge. He turns into a large parking lot that serves the back entrances to the library, post office, police station, Frank's Bar & Grille, the Fieldridge bakery, and a small fleet of high-rise apartments and condos. He drives into a parking space. She pulls in next to him.

He walks toward the line of buildings and, using a key, enters an unmarked door.

She follows him inside.

They go down a flight of stairs, and a room opens out in front of them, with a dozen partitioned offices and a separate office with a closed door.

Half a dozen people look up as they approach.

"Cabe." They nod, one at a time. He nods in response, and knocks lightly on the door to the office.

On the window, in black lettering, it says, "Captain Fran Komisky."

The door opens. A bronze-haired woman urges them to come in. Her hair is cropped short, and it frames her brown skin. She's wearing a black tailored skirt and jacket with a crisp white blouse. "Sit," she says.

They sit.

She sits behind her desk, which is littered with papers and has three phones and two computers resting on it.

The captain regards the two visitors for a moment. She rests her elbows on the desk, makes a tent with her fingers, and presses them against her mouth. Her eyes crinkle slightly with age.

She lowers her hands.

"So. Ms. Hannagan, is it? I'm Fran Komisky. Everybody calls me Captain." She leans over the desk and reaches for Janie's hand. Janie slips forward in her seat to shake it.

"Pleased to meet you, Captain," Janie says mechanically. She glances at Cabel. He's looking at his lap.

"Likewise," Captain says to Janie. "Cabe, you look

like hell. Shall we get this thing straightened out?"

"Yes, sir," Cabel says.

Janie looks up, wondering if Cabe means to call her that. It doesn't seem to bother the captain.

"Janie," she says in a tough voice. "Cabe here tells me he'd rather quit his job than lose you. Quite a young man he is, I must say. Anyway," she continues, "since that announcement affects me greatly, I've invited you here to discuss this little problem. And you need to know that I'd rather lose my left leg than lose Cabe at this stage of the game."

Janie swallows. Wonders what the hell is going on.

The captain looks at Cabe. "Cabe says you can be trusted with a secret. Is that true?"

Janie starts. "Yes, ma'am . . . sir," she says.

Captain smiles. Breaks the tension a bit.

"So. You're here because this dear boy has been lying to you, and I made him do it, and he's afraid you won't believe a word he says ever again. Ms. Hannagan, do you think you can believe me?"

Janie nods. What else can she do?

"Good. Somewhere I have a list of things I've jotted down, things I'm supposed to tell you, and I'll trust that if you have further questions, Cabel can answer them for you. And you'll believe him."

It sounds like an order.

Captain pages through the pile of papers and slips on half-glasses. Her phone rings, and she reaches automatically for a button, silencing it. "Here we are. First." She glances at Cabe, and then back at the paper. "Cabe is not 'involved' with Shay Wilder." She looks up, peering over her glasses. "I can't really prove that, Ms. Hannagan, but I've seen him nearly hurl after spending a recent evening with her. You good with that one?"

Janie nods. She feels like she's in somebody's weird dream.

"I said, are you good with that one?" Captain's voice booms.

"Yes, sir," Janie says. She sits up straighter in the chair.

"Good. Second. Cabe is not a drug dealer, pusher, liaison, user, and/or other in real life. He just plays one on TV." She pauses, but doesn't wait for a response this time.

"Third." She sits back, sets the paper on the desk, and taps a pen against her teeth. "We're this close"—she holds up her thumb and forefinger an inch apart—"to closing a major drug bust in North Fieldridge, up on the Hill. If this gets messed up because you whisper one word to anybody, and I mean anybody, I will hold you personally responsible, Ms. Hannagan. Besides Cabel and Principal Abernethy, you are the only one who knows about this. Are we clear?"

Janie nods, eyes wide. "Sir, yes, sir."

"Fine." Captain turns to Cabe. Her face softens. Slightly.

"Cabel," she says. "My dear boy. Are you with me or not? I need your head in the game. Now. Or this thing is shot to hell."

Cabel glances at Janie, and waits. She startles. He's leaving it up to her. She nods.

He sits up straight in his chair, looks Captain in the eye. "Yes, sir, I'm in the game."

Captain nods, and flashes an approving grin at both of them. "Good. Are we through here?"

Janie shifts uncomfortably.

And then she gives Cabel a haunting look.

"Fuck," she whispers, and digs her fingernails into the chair's armrests.

5:14 p.m.

Janie tumbles into a bank vault, where a black-haired cop sits on the floor, tied up. He wrestles with the ropes around his wrists and the gag in his mouth—

5:15 p.m.

She's back in the chair, next to Cabel, except Cabel is walking behind her, moving toward his chair again. The door is closed now. He sits down.

"Thanks," she whispers, and clears her throat. "Didn't see that one coming."

Captain is staring at her, eyes narrow. She looks from Janie to Cabel, back to Janie. She clears her throat. Loudly. Waiting.

Janie's face goes white.

Cabel's eyes go wide.

"Do you need medical assistance, Ms. Hannagan?" the captain finally says.

"No, sir. I'm fine, thank you."

"Cabe?"

"She's fine, sir."

Captain taps her pen on the desk, deliberating. She speaks slowly. "Is there anything else you two want to tell me about what just happened here?"

Cabel looks at Janie. "It's your call," he says quietly.

She hesitates.

Looks Captain in the eye.

"No, sir," she says. "Just . . . that . . . one of your officers is asleep at his desk and he's having a nasty dream. Looks like a bank robbery gone bad for the cops. He's tied up in a vault. Sir."

Captain's face doesn't change. She taps her lips with the pen now, and she's holding the wrong end. Blue ink leaves a tiny dotted trail under her nose.

"Which officer, Janie?" the captain asks slowly.

"I . . . I don't know his name. Short black hair. Early forties, maybe? Stocky. He was tied up with rope around his ankles and wrists, and had a white cloth gag around his mouth. Last I saw, anyway. Things change."

"Rabinowitz," Captain and Cabel say together.

"You want to double-check those facts for me, Cabe?"

"Sir, no offense, sir, but I don't need to. I think you might like to go question him yourself."

Captain tilts her head slightly, thinking. She pushes her chair back. "Don't go anywhere, you two," she says. She gives them both a strong, hard look before leaving. A look that says, "You better not fuck with me." When Captain opens the door and strides out, Janie grips the chair in anticipation. "Leave it open, Cabe," she gasps as she goes blind.

And she's back in the vault.

They're running out of air. The cop is struggling to get loose. He's trying to knock his cell phone out of his belt. Janie knows he wants to call his wife. She tries to get his attention. He looks into her eyes, and she concentrates on his pupils. *Ask me to help you,* she thinks as hard as she can think. Though she doesn't know how he will be able say it with the cloth stuffed in his mouth.

She hears a muffled plea and realizes it's good enough.

"Yes! That's it." She unwraps the gag, and realizes she spoke out loud. *Cool.* "Now." She stares into his eyes again. "This is your dream," she says. "You can change it. Get free."

He looks at her, his eyes wild.

"Get free," she encourages again.

He struggles and cries out.

And his arms and legs break free.

He lunges for his phone and calls 911. Closes his eyes, and the vault lock magically appears on the inside of the vault. A piece of paper floats down from nowhere with the information on how to open it.

He does it instantly.

And everything goes black.

5:19 p.m.

Janie's back with Cabel. He's touching her arm. "You okay, Hannagan?" He slips outside and returns, hands her a paper cup full of water, and she drinks it greedily.

She is shaking only slightly, from adrenaline more than anything. "I did it. I helped him," she says. "Oh, God, that was cool! My first time for a tough one like that." She grins.

Cabel is smiling wearily. "You'll have to explain that one later," he says. "If you're still speaking to me."

"Oh, Cabel. I . . ."

Captain comes back into the room and closes the door.

"Tell me what you saw, Ms. Hannagan. If you would, please. Rabinowitz says it's okay."

Janie blinks. She can't believe Captain is taking her seriously. She tells her everything she witnessed in the vault.

There is a long.

Long.

Pause.

"Hot damn," Captain says finally.

She tosses her half-glasses on the desk. "How'd you do that? You're . . . you're . . ."

She hesitates.

Continues, almost as if to herself, in a voice tinged with something. It might even be awe. "You're a regular Martha Stubin."

6:40 p.m.

Cabel and Janie are snarfing down grease-burgers and fries at Frank's Bar & Grille, next door to the police department. They sit at the counter on round red bar swivels, watching the cooks fry burgers five feet away. It's one of those old-fashioned places, where you can get a malted milk shake.

They eat with abandon, minds whirling.

8:04 p.m.

They are back at Cabel's house. Cabel shows her around the two rooms she hasn't seen: his bedroom and the computer room. He has two computers, three printers, a CB radio, and a police scanner.

"Unbelievable," she says looking around. "Wait—wait one second. . . . Do you live here alone?"

"I do now."

"How—"

"I'm nineteen. I was in the class ahead of you until ninth grade. You may remember."

Janie remembers him flunking into their class. "It was before I knew you," she remarks.

"My brother pops in now and then, just to see if I'm staying out of trouble. He and his wife live a few miles away. They moved out, thankfully, when I turned eighteen."

"Thankfully?"

"It's a really small house. Thin walls. Newlyweds."

"Ah. What about your parents?"

Cabel lounges on the couch. Janie sits in a chair

nearby. "My mom lives in Florida. Somewhere. I think." He shrugs. "Dad raised us. Sort of. I guess my brother actually raised me."

Janie curls up in her chair and watches him. He's far away. She waits.

"Dad was in Vietnam, at the tail end. His mind was messed up." Cabel looks at her. "When Mom left, he got mean. He pretty much beat the shit out of us. . . ." Cabel looks at the table. "He died. A few years ago. It's cool. Yanno? I'm over it. Done." Cabel gets up off the couch and stretches.

Janie stands up. "Take me back there," she says.

"What?"

"Show me. The back of the shed."

He bites his lip. "Okay . . ." He hesitates. "I haven't, you know. Been back there in a while. It was—used to be—my hiding place."

She nods. Gets her coat. Tosses his coat to him. They go out through the back door.

Crunch on the frosty grass.

Taste the air for snow.

When they get close, he slows down.

"You go ahead," he says. He stops at the edge of a small, dormant garden.

Janie looks at him. She's afraid. "Okay," she says. The grass grows long and squeaks as she walks through it.

Janie slips away into the darkness and disappears from Cabel's view behind the shed. She stops and peers at the shed, getting her eyes accustomed to the darkness. She sees her spot, where she leans against it in the dreams, and stands there.

Looks to the left.

Waits for the monster.

But she knows now that the monster died with his dad.

She crawls to the corner, to view the place where he comes from.

She sees it, vividly.

Cabel, leaving the house. Slamming the door.

The man on the steps, yelling. Following.

The punch to Cabel's face.

The lighter fluid to his belly.

The fire and screaming.

The transformation.

And the monster, running toward her, with knives for fingers. Howling.

She's starting to freak out, in the darkness.

Sucks in a breath.

Needs, desperately needs, to hear it was just a dream.

He's sitting on the back step. Quiet.

She walks to him. Takes his hand. Leads him inside.

The house is dark. She fumbles for a lamp, and in its glow, they cast shadows on the far wall. She closes the curtains. Takes his coat, and hers, and hangs them over the chairs in the kitchen, and he stands there, watching her.

"Show me," she says. Her voice shakes a little.

"Show you what? I think you've seen it all." His laugh is hollow, unsettled. Trying to read her mind.

She reaches up, unbuttons his shirt, slowly. He takes in a sharp breath. Closes his eyes for a minute. Then opens them. "Janie," he says.

His button-down is on the floor.

She pulls the T-shirt up. Just a little. She watches his eyes. He pleads to her with them.

Janie slips her fingers under his T-shirt. Touches the warm skin at the sides of his waist. Feels his shallow breathing quicken. Draws her hands upward.

Feels the scars.

He draws in a staggering breath and turns his head to the side. His lip shadow quivers on the wall. His Adam's apple bobs below it. "Oh, Christ," he says. His voice breaks. And he is shaking.

She lifts the shirt, pulls it over his head.

The burn scars are bumpy like peanut brittle. They pepper his stomach and chest.

She touches them.

Traces them.

Kisses them.

And he's standing there. Weeping. His hair floating up with winter static. His eyelashes, like hopping spiders in the dim light. He can't take it.

He bends forward.

Curls over like a sow bug.

Protecting himself.

Dropping to the floor.

"Stop," he says. "Please. Just stop."

She does. She hands him his shirt.

He mops his face with it.

Slips it back on.

"Do you want me to leave?" she asks.

He shakes his head. "No," he says, and shudders in gripping sobs.

She sits next to him on the floor, leaning against the couch. Pulls him to her. He lays his head in her lap and curls up on the floor while she pets his hair. He grips her leg like a teddy bear.

11:13 p.m.

Janie wakes him gently, fingers through his hair. She walks with him to his bedroom. Lies down beside him in his bed, just for a few minutes. Puts his glasses on his bedside table. Holds him. Kisses his cheek.

And goes home.

BUSTING OUT ALL OVER

December 6, 2005, 12:45 p.m.

She waits at his table in the library.

He meets her there.

"I have to work tonight," she whispers.

"After?" he asks.

"Yes. It'll be late."

"I'll leave the front door unlocked," he says.

She goes to her usual table.

And he designs a new dream, just for her.

6:48 p.m.

A man checks in at the front desk of Heather Home. He looks around, unfamiliar. She recognizes him, though he's tinged in gray now. Older. Lined.

"I'll show you," Janie says. She leads him to Mr. McVicker's room.

Knocks lightly on the door. Opens it.

Old Johnny McVicker turns toward the door.

Sees his son.

It's the first time in nearly twenty years.

The old man rises from his chair slowly.

Grabs hold of his walker.

His dinner tray and spoon clatters to the floor. But he doesn't notice. He's staring at his son.

Says, way too fast, "I was wrong, Edward. You were right. I'm sorry. I love you, son."

Edward stops in his tracks.

Takes off his hat. Scratches his head slowly.

Crumples the hat in his hands.

Janie closes the door and goes back to the desk.

11:08 p.m.

She parks her car at her house and sprints through the snow to his.

"I was wild," she says when she slips in the house. "You shoulda seen me with the bedpans."

He waited for her. And now he hugs her. Lifts her up. She laughs.

"Can you stay?" he asks. Begs.

"If I go home in the morning," she says. "Before school."

"Anything," he says.

Janie finishes up her homework, shoves it in her backpack, and finds him. He's sleeping. He's not wearing a shirt. She crawls into his bed and marvels silently at his stomach and chest. He breathes deeply. She settles in.

For now, anyway.

He knows she might have to go away.

Get away from his dreams, so she can sleep.

But when he dreams the fire dream, and meets her behind the shed, kisses and cries, begging for help, she reaches for his fingers in her blind, numb state and takes him with her into it, so he can watch himself.

She shows him how to change it.

It's your dream, she reminds him.

And she shows him how to turn the man on the step, the man who carries the lighter fluid and the cigarette, into the man on the step whose hands are empty, whose head is bowed. Who says, "I'm sorry."

When they both wake, the sun streams in the window.

It's 11:21 a.m. On a Wednesday.

They exclaim and laugh, loud and long. Because there's not one single parent between them who gives a damn.

Instead, they lounge on a giant beanbag in the computer room together, talking, listening to music.

They play truth or dare.

But it's all truth.

For both of them.

Janie: Why did you tell me you wanted to see me that first Sunday after Stratford, and then you didn't show?

Cabel: I knew I had to hit that party—I was going to come back early. I didn't know we were going to hold a fake bust. I got sent to jail overnight, just to make me look real. I was devastated. Captain let me out at six the next morning. That's when I left the note on Ethel.

Janie: Did you ever sell drugs?

Cabel: Yes. Pot. Ninth and tenth grade. I was, uh . . . rather troubled, back then.

Janie: Why did you stop?

Cabel: Got busted, and Captain made me a better deal.

Janie: So you've been a narc since then?

Cabel: I cringe at your terminology. Most narcs are young cops planted in schools to catch students. Captain had a different idea. She's not after the students, she's after the supplier. Who happens to be Shay's father. And she thought this was a good way to go—since he's starting to sell coke to kids at the parties. And implies he's got a gold mine somewhere. I've got to get him to say it on mic.

Janie: So you're a double agent?

Cabel: Sure. That sounds sexy.

Janie: You're sexy. Hey, Cabel?

Cabel: Yeah?

Janie: Did you really flunk ninth grade?

Cabel: No. (pause) I was in the hospital, most of that year.

Janie: (silence) And thus, the drugs.

Cabel: Yes . . . they helped with the pain. But then I got myself into a few, well, uh, situations. And Captain

stepped in my life at exactly the right moment before junior year, before I was too far in trouble. And it sounds weird, but she became sort of this army-type, no-nonsense mother I desperately needed. That was the Goth stage, where I decided I'd never get the girl of my dreams because of my scars. Not to mention the hairstyle.
(pause)
But then she slammed a door handle into my gut. And when a girl does that to a boy, it means she likes him.

Janie: (laughs)

Cabel: So that made me feel better. Because she didn't care what people thought if she spoke to me. Before I changed.
(pause)

Janie: (smiles) Why did you change it? Your look, I mean.

Cabel: Captain's orders. For the job. It's not my car, either, by the way. It's part of the image. I suppose I'll have to give it back after a while.
(pause)
Hey, Janie?

Janie: Yeah?

Cabel: What are you doing after high school?

Janie: (sighs) It's still up in the air, I guess. In two years, I've barely saved enough money for one semester at U of M . . . God, that's just crazy . . . so, unless I get a decent scholarship, it'll be community college.

Cabel: So you're staying around here?

Janie: Yeah . . . I, uh, I need to be close enough so I can keep an eye on my mother, you know? And . . . I think, with my little "problem," I'm going to have to live at home. Or I'll never get any sleep.

Cabel: Janie?

Janie: Yes?

Cabel: I'm going there. To U of M.

Janie: You are NOT.

Cabel: Criminal Justice. So I can keep my job here.

Janie: How do you know? Did you get an acceptance letter already? How can you afford it?

Cabel: Um, Janie?

Janie: Yesss, Cabel?

Cabel: I have another lie to confess.

Janie: Oh, dear. What is it?

Cabel: I do, actually, know what my GPA is.

Janie: And?

Cabel: And. I have a full-ride scholarship.

Cabel is pushed violently from the beanbag chair. And pounced upon. And told, repeatedly, what a bastard he is.

Janie is told that she will most certainly get a scholarship too, with her grades. Unless she plays hooky with drug dealers.

And then there is some kissing.

December 10, 2005

The weekend is shot. Cabel is back to courting Shay, and Janie is working Friday night, and Saturday and Sunday first shifts at the nursing home.

But Carrie finds Janie. And Janie, worried that the drug bust will go down over the weekend, really doesn't want Carrie mixed up in it. She asks Carrie if she wants to study for exams sometime. They reluctantly agree on Saturday night at Janie's.

Carrie shows up around six p.m., and she's already loaded. Janie makes her haul out her books and notes, anyway. "Are you gonna go to college or not?" she asks sharply.

"Well, sure," Carrie says. "I guess. Unless Stu wants to get married."

"Does he?"

"I think so. Maybe. Sometime."

"Do you?" Janie asks, after a moment.

"Sure, why not. Get me away from my parents."

"Your parents aren't that bad, really. Are they?"

Carrie grimaces. "You should have seen them before."

"Before what?"

"Before we moved in next door to you."

Janie hesitates. Trying to decide if this is the right time to ask. "Hey, Carrie?"

"What."

"Who's Carson?"

Carrie stares at Janie. "What did you just say?"

"I said, who is Carson?"

Carrie's face grows alarmed. "How do you know about Carson?"

"I don't. Otherwise, I wouldn't need to ask." Janie is walking a thin line here. One she can't see.

Carrie, obviously troubled, paces around the kitchen. "But how did you know to ask me about him?"

"You said his name once," Janie says carefully, "in your sleep. I was just curious."

Carrie sloshes some vodka in a glass. Sits down. Starts to cry.

Oh, shit, Janie thinks.

And then Carrie spills the story.

"Carson . . . was four."

Janie's stomach twists.

"He drowned. We were camping by a lake . . . it was . . ." Carrie trails off and takes a swallow of her drink. "He was my little brother. I was ten. I was helping Mom and Dad set up the campsite."

Janie closes her burning eyes. "Oh, shit, Carrie."

"He wandered down to the lake—we didn't notice. And he fell off the dock. We tried . . . we tried . . ." Carrie puts her face in her hands. Takes a long, shuddering breath. "We moved here a year later." Her voice turns quiet. "To start over. We don't talk about him."

Janie puts her arm around Carrie and hugs her. Doesn't know what to say. "I'm so sorry."

Carrie nods, and then whispers in a broken voice, "I should have watched him better."

"Oh, honey," Janie whispers. She holds Carrie close for a moment, until Carrie gently pulls away.

"It's okay." Carrie sniffles.

Janie, feeling completely helpless, fetches a roll of toilet paper from the bathroom. "I don't have any tissues . . . Carrie? Why didn't you ever tell me?"

Carrie wrings her hands. Blows her nose. Sniffles. "I don't know, Janers. I thought it would go away. I was so tired . . . so tired of being sad. I couldn't stand any more silent, pitying looks."

"Does Stu know?"

Carrie shakes her head. "I should probably tell him."

They are quiet for a long time.

"I guess maybe," Janie murmurs after a while, "the bad stuff never goes away. And it's nobody's fault."

Carrie sucks in a shivery breath and lets it out slowly. "Ah, well. We'll see, huh?" She smiles through the tears.

"Thanks, Janers. You're a really good friend." She pauses, and adds in a soft voice, "Just keep being normal now, okay? One sad look and I'm outa here, I swear to God."

Janie grins. "You got it. Kiddo."

December 11, 2005, 2:41 a.m.

When Carrie dreams, this time Janie knows what to do.

The forest, the river, the boy, drowning. Grinning.

Carrie, looking at Janie. Only a few minutes before the shark comes.

Carrie, crying out, "Help him! Save him!"

Janie concentrates, staring Carrie in the eyes. "Ask me, Carrie. Ask me."

He's bobbing and sinking, that eerie grin on his face.

"Help him!" she cries again to Janie.

Carrie! thinks Janie with all her might. *I can't help him. Ask me. Ask me to help . . . you.*

In the morning, Carrie remarks at breakfast, "I had the weirdest dream. It was one of these nightmares that I keep getting about Carson, but this time, it all changed and turned into this strange little . . . something. It was surreal."

"Yeah?" munched Janie. "Cool. Must be the feng shui over here or something."

"You think?"

"I dunno. Try rearranging your room, and then at night, tell yourself that you're going to change the nightmares from now on to work with your new harmonious surroundings."

Carrie gives her a suspicious look. "Are you yanking my chain?"

"Of course not."

December 12, 2005, 5:16 p.m.

Janie drives home slowly after a long afternoon at Heather Home. With the holidays on the way, the aides try to fit in some decorating in the schedule, along with their regular duties. And Janie managed to help three residents find some peace in their dreams. It was a decent day.

On a whim, she drives past Cabel's house, and is surprised to see his car in the driveway. She slows and pulls into the drive, leaving Ethel running.

She sprints to the front door and knocks briskly.

The door opens, and Cabel gives her a look. "Hey, Janie, what's up?" He's making signals with his eyes when Shay comes up from behind him and peers over his shoulder. She wraps her arms around his waist possessively.

"Hey, Janie," says Shay, a look of triumph in her eyes.

Janie grins, thinking fast. "Oh, hi, Shay. Sorry to disturb. Cabel, I'm wondering if you have those math notes you said I could borrow for tomorrow's exam?"

Cabel's eyes flash a message of gratitude. "Yeah," he says. "Be right back. You want to come in?"

"Nah. My shoes are wet from the snow."

Cabel reappears and hands her a bunch of papers, rolled up and secured in a rubber band. "We're heading out to a party now," he says, "But I kind of need these back tonight, since the exam's in the morning. How late can I stop by to get them?"

Shay bobs over his shoulder, intent on seeing and being seen. Janie notices Cabel has slowly straightened his posture and is standing at full height, and Shay has to jump to see past him. Janie masks a laugh. "I'll be up late, but I can put them in the mailbox for you before I go to bed. Thanks, Cabel. Have fun at the party, you guys! I'm sooo jealous."

Janie trots back to Ethel and heads for home, only a little melancholy over the scene she has just witnessed. She brings the notes in, changes her clothes, and gets out her books.

She pages through the papers Cabel gave her, hoping he didn't give her anything important, since she didn't actually need his stuff. In the middle of the pile, a scribbled note:

I miss you like crazy.
Love, Cabe.

She smiles, missing him. Wanting this mess to be over. She thinks about how he was willing to quit the job, wreck the months of progress the detectives had made, just to get things right with her.

Captain is right. He's a good guy.

Janie studies past midnight, partly hoping Cabe will come over. By one a.m., she's nodding over her work. She calls it a night and gathers Cabe's notes to put them in the mailbox. In case he comes for them. In case Shay is with him, and he has to pretend.

She writes a note and slips it inside the papers, then rolls them up and sets them outside in the mailbox.

She's happy she can sleep in, but checks her alarm clock twice to make sure it's set. The first exam starts at 10:30 a.m. tomorrow.

And she needs to ace it.

So she can get a scholarship.

Because without that, U of M is just an uncatchable dream.

December 13, 2005, 2:45 a.m.

When the phone rings, Janie jumps. She thinks it's the alarm clock for one confused moment, but by the fourth ring she's lunging for it.

Hoping it's Cabel.

Hoping he's standing outside, wanting to see her.

"Hello," she croaks, and clears the sleep from her voice.

She hears sniffling. "Janieeee," cries a voice.

"Who is this?"

"Janieee, it's me."

"Carrie? What's wrong? Where are you?"

"Oh fuck, Janie," Carrie mourns, "I'm so messed up."

"Where are you? Do you need a ride? Carrie, get it together, girl. Are you drunk?"

"My parents are gonna kill me."

Janie sighs.

Waits.

Listens to the sniffling.

"Carrie. Where are you."

"I'm in jail," she says finally, and the sobbing starts fresh.

"What? Right here in Fieldridge? What the hell did you do?"

"Can you just come get me?"

Janie sighs. "How much, Carrie?"

"Five hundred bennies," she says. "I'll pay you back.

Every cent. Plus interest. I promise, so much." She pauses. "Oh, and Janie?"

"Yessss?"

"Stu's here too." Janie can feel Carrie cringing through the phone.

Janie closes her eyes and runs her fingers through her hair. She sighs again. "I'll be there in thirty minutes. Stop crying."

Carrie gushes her thanks, and Janie cuts it short by hanging up.

Janie scrambles into her clothes and finds her stash of money that is waiting to be deposited into her college fund. She's twenty bucks short. "Shit," she mutters. She goes out of her room and runs into her mother, of all people.

"Was that the phone?" Her mother is bleary-eyed.

"Yeah . . ." Janie hesitates. "I gotta go get Carrie. She's in jail. Any chance . . . any chance you have twenty bucks to spare, Ma? I'll pay you back tomorrow."

Janie's mother looks at her. "Of course," she says. She goes into her room and comes out with a twenty. "You don't have to pay me back, honey."

If Janie had an extra hour to think about that little exchange, she might have come to the conclusion that there are one or two things more bizarre than falling into people's dreams.

3:28 a.m.

Janie climbs the steps to the front entrance of the police station and gets blown in through the door. It's snowing furiously. She looks around, and an officer waves her into the metal-detector area and through the security checkpoint. She recognizes him. It's Rabinowitz. She smiles, knowing he doesn't have a clue who she is.

"Through the doors. Cash or credit card payments only. No checks," he says, as if he's said it a billion times before.

Janie hears them before she pushes open the doors. There is a short line of sleepy-angry parents in front of her. Some of them are carrying on more pathetically than Carrie did on the phone. She peers around the corner and sees the bars of a holding cell.

She wonders if this is it. The bust. And then she sees Melinda, being escorted by a cop and her father. Her face is smudged in mascara and tears, and she looks terrible. Her father grabs her angrily by the arm and marches her out. Janie looks at the floor as Melinda goes past. She feels sorry for her.

The next three students she knows as well, and she can see their humiliation. Finally Janie is the last person standing at the desk. She sets one thousand dollars cash on the counter.

"Who you here for?" barks the guard.

"Carrie Brandt and Stu, ah . . ." She Googles her memory for his last name. "Gardner."

"I.D., please."

Janie pulls out her driver's license and hands it to the guard, who checks it closely.

He looks up at her for the first time.

"You're not eighteen."

Janie's stomach thuds. "No—not for another month," she says.

"Sorry, kid. Gotta be eighteen."

"But—" *Shit.*

The guard ignores her. She stands there. Thinking of all the things she knows but cannot reveal. She sighs and sits down in the chairs to think. She puts her head in her hands. Does she dare try to approach Rabinowitz, see if he'll vouch for her? But, no . . . Captain said not a word to anyone. That didn't exclude other cops.

"Can I at least go back there so she knows I tried?" Janie pleads.

The guard looks up. "You still here? All right, fine," he says. "Two minutes." Janie smiles gratefully and walks to the holding cell.

And she sees them. Sitting or lying on the benches.

Carrie and Stu. Huddled.

Shay Wilder and her brother. Looking extremely pissed, drunk, high, wasted, whatever.

Mr. Wilder. Looking fucked up in more ways than one.

And Cabe. Who is lounging on the bench like he lives there. And Shay, Janie notices gleefully, is as far away from Cabel as she can get.

She bites her lip.

Carrie rushes to the bars.

Janie looks at Carrie. "Honey," she whispers. "They won't let me. I'm not eighteen till next month. I'm working on it, though, okay? I promise. I'll figure something out, if I have to drag my own mother down here."

Carrie starts bawling. "Oh, it's so horrible being locked up in here," she whines.

Janie, who ran out of sympathy about a minute after the phone rang, just glares at Carrie. "Jeez, Carrie. Shut up already. Or I'm liable to leave you stranded."

"No!" chime the drunken voices of Shay, her brother, and Stu. Stu and Carrie start fighting.

Janie steals a glance at Cabel, who is watching her, the slyest of smiles on his face. He winks, and then nods, ever so slightly, in the direction of Mr. Wilder.

Janie looks.

He's leaning.

Falling.

Asleep.

She feels a rush of adrenaline. "I, uh, I gotta go back

up to the chairs, Carrie, but I'll get you out as soon as I can, okay?" Janie doesn't chance another look at Cabe.

She sits in the chairs nearest the holding cell, out of view of the guy at the front desk. She can just barely see Cabel's feet on the bench. His legs are crossed at the ankles. And she remembers him back when his jeans were too short, standing alone and greasy at the bus stop, less than two years ago.

She can hear Carrie and Stu arguing, and Shay and her brother raising their voices, telling her to get over herself and shut up—

And then she's whirling and blind, gripping the chair, hoping nobody walks by. She doesn't see Cabel stand up in the midst of the Carrie distraction and come to the edge of the cell bars, trying to catch her eye. Trying to tell her something.

She only sees what is in Mr. Wilder's hopes and fears. Or are they memories?

The dream intensifies and turns nightmarish. Janie is whipped around inside it.

Beaten, and blasted.

And she's trying to see everything. Everything. From the eyes and the mind of a criminal.

She doesn't see Cabel at all during that two-hour dream, pacing, burying his head in his hands. She doesn't see him watching her, horrified, as she's falling sideways off the chair, deadweight. Slamming her face on the corner of the coffee cart.

6:01 a.m.

Her head is pounding.

She's clammy. Cold.

Her face slides in blood on a cold tile floor.

She thinks her eyes are open, but her vision is taking a long time to return.

She can't move her body.

In the distance, she hears Cabel, calling her name, calling the guard.

Carrie is screaming.

For Janie, everything is black as night.

6:08 a.m.

Janie is being lifted onto a stretcher. She concentrates. Tries to wake up. Her head pounds.

They wheel her out into the hallway of the police station.

"Stop," she croaks.

Clears her voice, and says it again.

"Stop."

Two paramedics look down at her. She opens her eyes. Only one wants to. But she can see shadows.

"I'm fine," she says, and struggles to sit up. "I get seizures now and then. I'm fine. See?"

She holds her hands out to show them how fine she is.

And sees the blood.

Her eyes grow wide as she strains for her vision to return in full.

She feels her face. The blood is dripping, streaming, from her eyebrow onto her lashes.

"Aw, fuck," she says. "Listen, don't you just have some Steri-Strips? Seriously."

The paramedics look at each other, and back at her.

She tries a different tactic. "I don't have any insurance, guys. I can't afford this. Please."

One of the medics wavers. "It's Janie, right? Listen, you were in a complete spasm on the floor. Rigid. Unconscious. You smacked your head on the corner of a rusty metal coffee cart."

Janie wheedles them. "I'm up-to-date on my tetanus shot. Look, I've got a math exam in—soon, and my college future rides on it. I'm telling you, I'm refusing treatment. Now let me off of here."

Slowly, the paramedics back off so she can get down. She swings her heavy, unfeeling legs over the side of the stretcher just as Captain Komisky breezes through the security check.

"What the hell is going on down here?" she asks brightly. "Why, hello, Ms. Hannagan. Are you coming or going?"

Janie looks around on the stretcher and grabs a hunk of gauze, trying to find the source of the blood. "I'm working my way off this thing any second now," Janie mutters.

She takes a deep breath.

Hops off the edge.

Sticks the landing like ol' what's her name in the Olympics.

Captain is watching her, an amused look on her face. She offers Janie her arm. "Come, dear," she says. "Looks like you've been busy tonight." She waves the paramedics away with a sweeping gesture, and they go like lightning.

Janie smiles gratefully and holds the gauze to her eye. Her sweatshirt is stained with blood. She feels like she's wearing cement shoes, and her head feels like a balloon.

"I called on my way in, got the scoop," she explains when the paramedics are gone. "I wonder if we need to have a chat in my office?"

"I—sure. Um, what time is it?" Janie forgot to put her watch on when she left the house, and she's lost without it.

"Six fifteen, or thereabouts," Captain says. "I imagine Mr. Strumheller has had enough by now, don't you?"

Janie is having trouble concentrating. She knows she needs to eat. She gives a shaky laugh. "I suppose that's up to you, sir," she murmurs.

And then she remembers.

Carrie and Stu.

"Captain," she says nervously. "I came down here a few hours ago trying to spring my friend and her boyfriend. I've got the bail money, but I'm not eighteen until next month. Any chance you can—"

"Of course."

Janie sighs, relieved. "Thank you."

"Before we go in," Captain says, "let's remember that you don't know me. Right?"

"Yes, sir," she says.

"Good girl. Go get your friends."

6:30 a.m.

Carrie rushes out of the holding cell like it's filling up with poison gas. Stu follows. Carrie sees Janie covered with blood and nearly passes out, but both Stu and Janie ignore her dramatics.

"You guys are gonna have to walk. I'm sorry," Janie says firmly. "I have to fill out some dumb paperwork for an incident report or something." She points to her eye and makes like it's the last thing she wants to do. She shakes her head, pretending to be pissed. "Stupid cops."

Stu squeezes Janie's shoulder. "Thank you, Janie." He gives her a grateful look. "You're a good friend. To both of us."

Janie smiles, and Carrie looks abashed. "Thanks, Janers," she says.

"I'm glad you called me, Carrie," Janie says. *Now, go away.*

6:34 a.m.

Janie heads to the restroom, bloodying gauze pressed against her rapidly swelling eyebrow. She checks the mirror. The cut is beautiful in its own right. It lies just below her brow line, from the arch to where the brow tapers, and is straight and clean. One day, she might wish she'd gotten stitches. But as scars go, it's in a perfectly sexy spot.

She turns her sweatshirt inside out to hide the ridiculous amount of blood that oozed from the inch-long gash, and washes her face and hands. She takes a handful of brown paper towels, wets them, and puts the pressure back on it. Then she slurps water from the faucet.

6:47 a.m.

Janie leaves the restroom, and Cabel is there, pulling her into the cloakroom area. He looks tired. And relieved to see her.

"Let me see," he says.

She pulls the paper towels away and shows him her war wound.

"It's very impressive," he says, and then grows serious, his deep brown eyes betraying his concern. "When I saw you about to go down, I—" He stops and sighs. "I watched you. Most of that two hours, whenever I could pull it off without looking suspicious. It made me crazy that I couldn't get to you."

Janie, who is now shivering and getting very light-headed, just leans against him.

He strokes her back, rests his chin on her head. "You sure you're up for a chat with the boss?" he asks.

Janie nods against his chest.

"I'll get you something to eat just as soon as we get out of here, okay?"

She smiles. "Thanks, Cabe."

"Meet me at the back entrance, okay? You remember which door? We need to split up."

"Yeah, okay, good thinking," she murmurs. Cabel walks nonchalantly to a staircase and goes down. Janie heads out the front entrance and walks half a block through the blizzard to get around to the back of the shops and buildings. When she gets to the unmarked door, she's in a cold sweat. She knocks lightly. It opens, and she follows Cabel down the stairs.

The place is buzzing, and Cabel takes a few slaps on the back and swipes upside the head for his overnight work. "We're still not there yet," he says modestly.

He knocks on the captain's door, and she hollers, "Come." Cabel and Janie slip inside.

"You two have exams today, no? Do we have time for this right now?"

"Ten thirty, Captain. We've got plenty of time."

Captain looks at Janie closely. "Jesus, Mary, and Joseph," she says. "You're gonna have a heck of a shiner by the time the day's over. Did you black out?"

"I . . . uh . . ." Janie shrugs. "I really have no idea."

"Yes, I think she did." Cabel cuts in. "I'm going to need to watch her all day. And probably all night, too," he adds. Very, very seriously.

The captain throws a rubber eraser at him and sends him out for coffee. "And get this poor girl some rations, while you're at it, before she breaks in half." She opens her desk drawer and fishes around in it. Pulls out a first-aid kit and tosses a bag of airline peanuts on the desk as well. "Slide in over here, will you?" she says. Janie scoots her chair around the side of the desk.

"Jesus," Captain mutters again, and spreads a liberal amount of antibiotic cream over the cut. She rips open a package of Steri-Strips and neatly and quickly closes the cut. "That's better," she says. "If your mother and/or father have any questions about what happened to you, have them give me a call. I'd appreciate a heads-up if you think they're likely to sue." She slides the bag of peanuts across the desk to Janie. "Eat."

"Yes, sir," she says gratefully, ripping open the package. "You won't hear from anyone."

Cabel returns with three coffees, a small cup of milk,

and a bag full of muffins and doughnuts. He casually sets the milk and bran muffin in front of Janie and pours three creams and three sugars into her coffee.

She drinks the milk, her hand shaking, and feels the ice-cold goodness of it going all the way down. "Excellent," she says, and takes a deep breath.

"So," begins Captain. "You have a report for me, Cabel?"

"Yes, sir. We arrived at the party at nineteen-ten hours, marijuana already in progress, and by twenty-three-thirty, the coke was on the glass. Five minors and several adults snorted lines. Mr. Wilder took me aside, and we discussed our partnership, he being rather pleased at the turnout. He was semicoherent but stoned, and he told me he had a stash he was ready to quote 'put on the market'—his words. Apparently that was enough for Baker and Cobb, though I'm pissed we don't have the actual location of the stash. They arrived within three minutes and broke the place up, taking only those who were too stupid to go peacefully. And, of course, Mr. Wilder and his two children. Mrs. Wilder wasn't present. And I really don't think she's mixed up in it." He glances sideways at Janie and shrugs an apology. "Carrie was really toasted and put up a huge fight. Sorry about that."

Janie smiles. "Maybe the experience will knock some sense into her," she says.

"By two a.m., we were all in what I like to call my

little home away from home," Cabel continues. "Janie here came in to try to bail Carrie and her boyfriend out, and as luck would have it, Mr. Wilder was fucked up enough to fall asleep in the din. Janie settled in for the ride." He sits back, finished with his report.

Captain nods. "Good work, Cabe, as always." She turns to Janie. "Janie. A disclosure. You weren't hired by us, and we didn't ask you to help in this investigation. You have no obligation to share what happened before you creamed your face on our lovely piece of shit coffee cart, which I'm tossing in the Dumpster right after this meeting. But if you wish to, and you feel you have anything pertinent to add, I'd welcome it." She scribbles something on a notepad and puts it in her pocket, and then she continues. "Sounds like Cabe's a little perturbed that we don't have the location of the cake, and I personally would like to have that piece of information so we can go for the maximum sentence. Any chance you picked up something along those lines?" She chuckles quietly at her own pun. "Take your time, dear."

Janie, thinking more clearly now, runs through Mr. Wilder's nightmare in her head. She closes her eyes at one point and shakes her head, puzzled. Then looks up.

"This might sound silly, but do the Wilders own a yacht?"

"Yes," Cabel says slowly. "It's in storage someplace for the winter. Why?"

She is quiet for a long time. She doesn't quite trust her intuition enough to say it, even though she knows she has nothing to lose.

"Orange life jackets?" she says hesitantly.

Captain leans forward, intrigued, and her voice is less harsh than usual. "Don't be afraid to be wrong, Janie. A lead's a lead. Most of them turn out wrong, but no crime gets solved without 'em."

Janie nods. "I'll spare you the endless dream unless you want to hear it all. But the major part that sticks out to me, and kept repeating, is this:

"We're on a yacht, and it's sunny and beautiful on the ocean. What looks like a gorgeous tropical island is in the distance, and Mr. Wilder is heading for it. Mrs. Wilder is sunning herself on the deck of the yacht—at the front end, you know? And then suddenly, the weather turns cloudy and windy, and a storm hits, slamming into the boat, I mean hard, like a hurricane, with the wind . . ."

She pauses, closes her eyes, and she's in it. In a trance. "And Mr. Wilder is getting frantic, because every time he gets close to the shore of this island, one of those backward waves pushes us out farther. Like in that one movie, where Tom Hanks is that castaway dude on that island with his pet volleyball?"

Cabe chuckles. "I think it's called *Cast Away*, Hannagan."

"Yeah. Whatever. Meanwhile, Mrs. Wilder is still sitting on the deck, reading a book, oblivious to the storm. Weird, I know. He calls to her to get inside the cabin and get the life jackets out, but she can't hear him. And then the yacht starts spinning and slams into the reef, and we're all flying out into the water. The yacht is in smithereens, and all the stuff that was inside the cabin is floating around, being carried by waves.

"Mrs. Wilder is flailing and drowning in the water, and Mr. Wilder swims around picking things up out of the water. He sees his wife struggling, and he grabs life jackets—there are at least fifteen of them floating here and there, and he's got maybe eight or nine of them strung on his arms. He starts to swim toward her. . . ."

Janie closes her eyes and swallows. Her voice is shaking. "And I think, he's going to save her. . . ."

Cabel bites his lip.

Captain offers her a break.

She waves her hand, trying not to lose concentration, and continues.

"He starts to swim toward her with life jackets. But instead of saving her, he says . . . um . . . he says, 'You can rot in hell, you old bitch.' And then he swims past her, toward the shore, with all those life jackets." She takes a breath. "Like they are the most important thing in his life. And . . ."

She pauses.

Continues in an odd voice. "And the jackets, they aren't floating anymore—they're dragging in the water. Sinking. Pulling him down. Under. And he won't let go."

Janie opens her eyes and looks solemnly at Captain. "I think the packages you're looking for might just be sewn inside the life jackets, sir."

Captain is already dialing the phone trying to get a search warrant for the yacht.

Cabel's mouth hangs open.

Janie's head throbs. "Do you have any Excedrin?" she whispers.

10:30 a.m.

Janie and Cabel sit down for their math exam.

10:55 a.m.

Janie, parched, salty tears running silently down her cheeks, closes her blank blue book, stands up, turns it in, and walks out of the classroom, every eye in the room staring at her as she goes. Cabel scribbles a few more answers, waits a few minutes, and turns his in too. Initially, he looks in the parking lot for her and, seeing her car being slowly covered in the snowstorm, breathes a sigh of relief she's not out driving in this mess. He goes back inside the school and searches the rooms.

He finds her, finally, passed out on her table in the empty library.

Picks her up.

Takes her to the emergency room.

On the way, he calls Captain. Tells her what's going on. Suggests maybe now's not a good time for Janie to get stuck in the dreams of random hospital visitors.

When they arrive at the ER, they're ushered to a private room. Cabel grins. "I love this job," he murmurs.

Janie is dehydrated. That's all.

They give her an IV, and then Cabel takes her to his house. She sleeps a long time. He sleeps too, on the couch.

She blames it on the salty sea.

GLORY AND HOPE

December 16, 2005, 4:30 p.m.

Cabel and Janie sit in Captain's office.

Captain comes in.

Closes the door.

Sits down behind her desk and takes a sip of coffee. Crosses her legs. Leans back in her chair and looks at the two teenagers.

"We got it," she says. She smiles, and then laughs like she won the lottery.

And shoves an envelope toward Janie.

Inside:

a contract

a scholarship offer

a paycheck

"Read it over. Let me know if you're interested," Captain says.

And pauses.

"Good work, Janie."

December 25, 2005, 11:19 p.m.

Janie swipes the last bit of frosting from the cake at Heather Home, walks the rounds, says silent good-byes to the sleeping residents, and gives the director a grateful hug. She takes a red helium balloon from the cake table, turns, and walks out the door for the last time, slowly now, through the parking lot to Ethel.

Drives to her house, and sprints through the snow to his.

Opens the door.

Slips in.

He's waiting, in his sleep, for her.

She slides into the dark shadow against his body. She kisses his shoulder. He takes her hand. Strings his fingers through hers. Holds on tightly.

And they are off, through the link of fingers.

Watching themselves, together.

Catching his dreams.

STILL AWAKE?
THERE'S MORE:

FADE

1:42 a.m.

Janie dreams in black and white.

She's walking down Center at dusk. The weather is cool and rainy. Janie's been here before, though she doesn't know what town she's in. She looks around excitedly at the corner by the Dry Goods store, but there is no young couple strolling arm in arm there.

"I'm here, Janie," comes a soft voice from behind. "Come, sit with me."

Janie turns around and sees Miss Stubin seated in her wheelchair next to a park bench along the street.

"Miss Stubin?"

The blind old woman smiles. "Ah, good. Fran has given you my notes. I've been hoping for you."

Janie sits on the park bench, her heart thumping. She feels tears spring to her eyes and quickly blinks them away. "It's good to see you again, Miss Stubin." Janie slips her hand into Miss Stubin's gnarled fingers.

"Yes, there you are, indeed." Miss Stubin smiles. "Shall we get on with it, then?"

Janie's puzzled. "Get on with it?"

"If you are here, then you must have agreed to work with Captain Komisky, as I did."

"Does Captain know I'm having this dream?" Janie is confused.

Miss Stubin chuckles. "Of course not. You may tell her if you wish. Give her my fond regards if you do. But I'm here to fulfill a promise to myself. To be available to you, just as the one who taught me remained with me until I was fully prepared, fully knowledgeable about what my purpose was in life. I'm here to help you as best I can until you no longer need me."

Janie's eyes widen. *No!* she thinks, but she doesn't say it. She hopes it takes a very long time before she no longer needs Miss Stubin.

"We'll meet here now and then as you go through my case files and learn from my notes. When you have questions about my notes, return here. I trust you know how to find me again?"

Janie's eyes widen. "Yes . . . you mean, direct myself to dream this again?"

Miss Stubin nods.

"Yes, I think I can do that. I'm sort of out of practice," Janie says sheepishly.

"I know you can, Janie." The old woman's curled fingers tighten slightly around Janie's hand. "Do you have an assignment from Captain?"

"Yes. We think there's a teacher who is a sexual predator at Fieldridge High."

Miss Stubin sighs. "Difficult. Be careful. And be creative—it may be tricky to find the right dreams to fall into. Keep up your strength. Be prepared for every opportunity to search out the truth. Dreams happen in the strangest places. Watch for them."

"I . . . I will," Janie says softly.

Miss Stubin cocks her head. "I must go now." She smiles and fades away, leaving Janie alone on the bench.

2:27 a.m.

Janie's eyes flutter and open. She stares at the ceiling in the dark and then flips on her bedside lamp.

Scribbles the dream in her notebook. *Wow,* she thinks. *Cool.*

BUT WAIT, THERE'S MORE!

Lisa McMann presents Janie—the way Cabel sees her . . .

October 14, 2005, 10:05 a.m.

"Good luck," he says, his voice harsh. Cabel Strumheller shoves his way past classmates and off the bus, and enters the hotel in Stratford, Canada. Fuming. Still shaking a little. Eyes to the ground, not wanting to accidentally look at her, see if she's coming.

He goes straight to his room and flops on the bed, staring at the ceiling. Three other guys let themselves in. They rummage around the room for a few minutes, but Cabe barely looks at them, barely acknowledges their presence. They don't talk to him, either. What else is new?

Once his weekend roommates are gone, off to see the first play, Cabel rolls over on the hotel bed to think about things.

About Janie Hannagan, and what exactly happened on the bus for the past four hours.

About what the hell is wrong with her, and how she managed to get inside his dream.

He slams his fist in the pillow. Can't get the nightmare to stop.

Cabel stands on the steps at the back door of his house, hand on the knob of the open door, looking in. Then he slams it shut and marches through the dry, yellow grass. His dad bursts out the door after him, yelling, standing on the step, carrying a beer and a cigarette in one hand, a can of lighter fluid in the other. His dad screams at him, and Cabel turns, frightened of the towering man. He freezes as his father approaches. The man sprays Cabe's clothes with the lighter fluid.

Sets Cabe on fire.

Cabel flops around on the ground in flames, screaming, pain searing through him, the fire blistering his skin. And then, with a furious roar, he transforms into an enormous monster with knives for fingers and he lunges for his father with only one goal in mind.

Killing him.

That's how it starts—the nightmare Cabe has had for years. That, or some form of it. It changes a bit each time. Cabel can't imagine a worse nightmare.

But that's not even the part that's bothering him. Not now. He's packed away all those emotions, thank you very much. That nightmare he can handle.

But what happened on the bus? That was just crazy. Because this time, asleep sitting next to Janie, he actually watched himself have the nightmare. As if he were an onlooker to someone else's dream.

And Janie was there, too, behind the shed in the backyard with Cabel.

Watching.

Watching Cabel's dream play out as if they were right there, in it.

And then afterward, when he woke up, seeing the shock in her face too—it was like a confession, and she didn't try to deny it.

He knows her. Knows where she lives. Casually, not weird like a stalker or anything. They'd ridden the bus together since middle school, back when Cabe was a grade ahead of her. Back before his dad messed up Cabe's life.

But Cabe doesn't want to think about that now. Doesn't want to think about his dad ever again. He's done with that. Done with him.

Still, the nightmare he had on the bus is fresh. He didn't think he was still having that one. But now he knows he has been.

And he's not the only one who knows that.

The monster man roars and runs away from the house, back toward the shed. There's a girl back there. Janie. The girl he always dreams about.

The monster man growls. He sees her.

She squeaks and closes her eyes, her back pressed up against the shed, as if she's trying to melt into the siding.

And then the monster transforms, back into Cabel. He looks at the girl, so sorry, so very sorry for scaring her. Wanting her to see him like nobody else ever does. The guy that nobody really knows. When she opens her eyes and sees him, she steps toward him.

He touches her face.

Leans in.

Kisses her.

She kisses him back.

"Ugh," he says, remembering how the nightmare ends. Squeezes his eyes shut, trying to figure it out. Trying to understand how Janie Hannagan managed to see all of that.

"She's a freak," he says slowly. "Psychotic. What if she's an alien?" Cabe shakes his head. He's seen enough weird stuff to know that weird stuff really happens. Not much surprises him anymore. And after what just happened, thinking Janie might be an alien or at the very least, psychic, isn't much of a stretch. Is she dangerous, though? He thinks she might be.

He feels the paranoia coming, lets it wash over him. Was she spying on him? How long has she known that he dreams about such awful things? And that he dreams about her? It's embarrassing. And now, quite possibly, after four hours riding together in the freaking middle of the night, she knows the dreams and nightmares of half the people on that bus.

But why are they oblivious when he's not? Why aren't they confronting her?

Is he just imagining this?

He can't figure it out.

He caught Janie's eye once or twice after that, and she didn't look away in disgust or anything. But they didn't speak.

When the homecoming dance approached, Cabe thought fleetingly about asking her. Ha. Yeah, right. No way she'd go with him. He was a total loser. The only group that accepted him was the Goths. And they take anyone.

He almost didn't even go to the dance, but the guys were going to hang out, so what the hell, right? He never even went inside the gym. He just loitered outside the back door with the guys, smoking, and thinking about how he should quit now that he was getting his life figured out. And wondering if Janie was inside.

When the door flew open, nobody saw it coming. The doorknob gutted him before his foot could stop it. Took his breath away for a minute. Searing pain. He doubled over. His friends laughed. Why not? It was funny for them, he supposed.

But his eyes stayed on her as she flew out of there as if on a mission in the dark, cool evening, heading down the same street Cabe had walked dozens of times a year, every time he missed the bus.

She wobbled on high heels like she'd never worn them before. It was a long walk home, and not very pleasant—it was getting cold and the farther away from school, the worse the neighborhood got. Once Cabe got his breath back, he eyed his skateboard. Maybe now was his chance. He adjusted his beanie, shoved his bangs up under it a little so he could

He saw her on that bus. For hours, on and off, she shook. Out of control, like a multitude of seizures. She'd begged him to keep quiet about it after the first episode, made him promise her he wouldn't get help, wouldn't tell a soul, no matter how many more times it happened. He saw how she was too weak to get food when they stopped at McDonald's. Watched her helplessly. She looked terrible. Would anybody subject herself to that on purpose?

But she got inside his psyche, where nobody else could ever go. Where he doesn't *want* anybody to go. And it's scary. What *is* she?

He hasn't felt this vulnerable in a long time.

Cabel shakes his head.

He thinks about the first time she noticed him at the neighborhood bus stop on the first day of junior year. It was funny then—they'd ridden the same bus for a few years, but he'd never seen her even glance his way.

He'd heard what Carrie Brandt had said to Janie back then while they waited for the bus to come. *Lookie, it's your boyfriend.* And Carrie laughed. God, that was embarrassing. Janie shushed Carrie, but then she started laughing too.

Cabe sat behind them on the bus to school that day. Pretended to sleep so he could overhear. In case they were going to make fun of him even more.

But they didn't.

Not Janie. Not ever again.

see. Lit another cigarette and smoked it slowly, his fingers shaking just a little.

"You going after her?" one of the guys, Jake, asked him.

"Maybe," Cabe said coolly. He took another drag and let it out slowly, then crushed the butt with his shoe and grabbed his board. "Yeah."

"I'm coming," another guy said. "Curfew."

"Me too," said another.

Cabe took a breath and frowned in the dark. "Whatever."

Before he could change his mind, he tucked his board under his arm and they set out.

It took several minutes to catch up to her on foot, and for a short time he thought he'd lost her. She'd abandoned the high heels by now, but the neighborhood was deteriorating rapidly as they moved toward the crappy side of town, where both Cabel and Janie lived.

He saw her tense up as the three approached. The two guys laid their boards down and she froze. Cabel cursed under his breath. He didn't mean to freak her out.

"Jeez!" she said. Recognizing him, thankfully. "Scare a girl half to death, why don't you." She looked pissed.

Cabe shrugged. Outwardly cool, inwardly a mess. His gut twisted and churned. *What the hell am I doing?* But it was too late to go back now. He tried desperately to think of something to say. The other guys skated up ahead, giving him some distance.

"Long walk," he said. Cringed at how lame it was. "You, uh"—his voice cracked—"okay?"

"Fine," she said, clipping the word. "You?"

Cabel gulped. He took a deep breath. No idea what to do next. But he could hardly stand to watch her walk barefoot. She was limping already.

"Get on," he said, and put the board down on the ground. Took Janie's shoes from her hand. "You'll rip your feet to shreds. There's glass an' shit."

Janie stopped. Looked at him. And he could see something in her tough-girl face. Vulnerability or something. It made his stomach twist.

"I don't know how," she said.

He grinned, then. Relieved. She didn't tell him to get lost. Definitely a step in the right direction. "Just stand. Bend. Balance," he said. "I'll push you."

And, after staring at him for a long minute, she did it. Unbelievable. He placed his hand gently on the small of her back, hoping that was okay with her, but not about to ask. Pushed her, and after a few wobbles, she figured out how to stand without falling and tilt the board to steer as he pushed her through the crappy streets of South Fieldridge.

He hadn't felt this good about himself in a long time. And even though he couldn't think of anything to say, it was okay, there in the dark. The two of them, awkward, silent. The warmth of her back on his hand in the chilly evening. The fact that she trusted him. That she wasn't afraid. That she didn't run away screaming. She let him touch her, for crying out loud.

Incredible.

He hardly noticed when the other guys took off, heading to their respective homes. It was all he could do to keep his concentration on avoiding stones and glass.

When he pushed her up her driveway to the step, he knew it was over. For the moment, at least. But it was enough for now. It was hope.

Janie hopped off the skateboard and opened the screen door.

He set her shoes on the step, hesitated for a moment, then picked up his board and left her there without a word. Just a nod. Totally at a loss.

He was at the road when he heard it. "Thanks, Cabel." Her voice was thin, soft in the air. "That was sweet."

Freaking music, it was. Enough to make a guy a little bit crazy inside.

Cabel thinks about that day a lot lately.

He sits back up on the hotel bed and then goes into the bathroom. Splashes water on his face and just leans over the sink, his head butting up against the mirror, thinking. Thinking about how, back then, he had no idea just how complicated this thing was going to get.

3:13 p.m.

While the rest of the seniors of Fieldridge High are at the theatre watching *Camelot*, Cabel wanders the hotel, then heads outside and walks to the nearby shopping mall. He takes in a movie—it's a tough call choosing between *Capote* and *Return of the Living Dead 5*, but after the nightmare on the bus, horror is not sounding good today.

He grabs dinner at the mall's food court and hangs around the music store until he gets kicked out for looking like a no-good teenager. What is it with adults anyway? They're so scared and suspicious all the time. *Hell,* Cabe thinks, *we're just trying to get by, like them.*

He wanders down to the Chapters bookstore and browses the sci-fi and fantasy section. Thinks this whole thing with Janie and the nightmares feels a little sci-fi, too.

And then he pauses.

Looks around the store, and moves to the self-help section.

When he sees a shelf of books on dreams, he grabs a few, finds a chair, and settles in. Hours go by as he reads, studies. Fascinated. At closing time, Cabel purchases the books. He walks through the darkness back to the hotel.

He pretends to be asleep when the guys come in after eleven from the theatre. Doesn't want to answer any questions about where he's been all day. Besides, his brain is full. He's exhausted and still confused. Troubled. But his anger is fading.

It doesn't seem like Janie can help it, or she would have tried to hide it on the bus. That's the conclusion he comes to, anyway.

He drifts off to sleep.

October 15, 2005, 4:03 a.m.

Cabel's in a shopping mall. In the center courtyard, there is a kiosk with a short line of people. He gets in line behind the others. Sees a giant wooden box on the floor. Two people climb in and lie down. The vendor running the kiosk closes the top on them, and then pushes a button. The box slowly descends into the floor as the line of people watch in silence.

"What's happening?" Cabel whispers to the person in front of him.

"It's a game," the girl says. She turns to look at him, and Cabel realizes it's Janie.

"Like a virtual ride or something?"

"Sort of."

Cabel shrugs and watches. The box surfaces once again and the lid opens. Only one person gets out—a sobbing woman. She points to the box and cries out, "He's dead!"

Immediately the paramedics are there. They remove the dead man and the kiosk worker signals for the next people in line to get into the box.

"This is not cool," Cabel says to Janie.

"It is what it is," Janie says.

The next couple goes down and when they surface, the man gets out. He is sobbing, pointing. "She's dead!" he cries out. People have to help him walk away.

Cabel's sweating now. "Come on, Janie," he says. "Let's go."

"We can't," she says. "If you get in the line, you must stay for the ride. See?" she points to a sign that says exactly that.

Soon it is their turn.

"Please, Janie," Cabel pleads. "Come on! We can just go. Do you see what's happening?"

"We can't control what's happening, Cabel," she says. She

looks at him with sorrow in her eyes. "There's no controlling it. It is what it is."

The kiosk worker signals Janie and Cabel to enter the box. Up close, Cabel can see it's lined, like a coffin.

"No, Janie—no. We don't have to do this!"

Janie gives Cabel a sorrowful look. She hesitates, and then she says, "It's okay. You stay. I'll go." And then she squeezes Cabel's hand, brushes his cheek with her fingertips. Smiles a sad, crooked smile.

Cabel watches her step into the coffin. "Wait! What will happen?" But he already knows.

Janie waves. "It's okay," she says, sincere. "It would have been me anyway."

The kiosk worker closes the lid on Janie.

Cabel is frantic, watching the box being lowered. "Stop!" he cries. "Stop! Let me in!"

But it's too late. Cabel lunges for the box as it disappears into the floor. Cabel falls to the tile, unable to speak or scream or cry. Finally he gasps. "Coward!" he says to himself. "Janie, no! Come back! I'm sorry!"

The wait is endless, but finally the box returns to the surface. The lid opens.

Janie is dead.

Cabel rolls over in the bed. "No," he whispers.

4:55 a.m.

He sits up. "Sheesh," he says, awake now. He looks at the clock, disoriented. Forgets for a moment where he is. The other guys in the room are sleeping soundly. Cabel takes a deep breath and settles back down on the pillow. He feels his heart still racing. Tells himself to calm down, and after a while, he does. But he can't get back to sleep. Finally, he dozes off again, restless.

8:24 a.m.

Cabe ignores the others as they get ready for a final session of Shakespeare before everyone heads back to Fieldridge High. When they are gone, he takes a long shower and slowly gets ready for the day. Thinking. Thinking about Janie. About the dream. About all sorts of things and how they relate to his life . . . and to Janie's, too, probably. Shame. Disappointment. Loneliness.

He pulls up the comforter and sits down on top of it, trying to figure her out. And knowing that even though he doesn't understand her, he needs to know what happened . . . and what could happen. There's no way he can just let her go or keep silent, like he did on the skateboard night. No way he can look at her again without demanding answers.

11:31 a.m.

Cabe hops up off the bed, hungry and resolved, and grabs his jacket. Slips his shoes on. Thinks about what Janie must be going through right now, this minute. Wonders if she skipped the morning play to catch up on sleep. He imagines her, stuck in a room with three other girls and their collective dreams all night. He's sure Janie really needs food by now.

And . . . well.

It's not going to deliver itself.

Read ahead for an excerpt from Lisa McMann's

crash

One

My sophomore psych teacher, Mr. Polselli, says knowledge is crucial to understanding the workings of the human brain, but I swear to dog, I don't want any more knowledge about this.

Every few days I see it. Sometimes it's just a picture, like on that billboard we pass on the way to school. And other times it's moving, like on a screen. A careening truck hits a building and explodes. Then nine body bags in the snow.

It's like a movie trailer with no sound, no credits. And nobody sees it but me.

Some days after psych class I hang around by the door of Mr. Polselli's room for a minute, thinking that if I have a mental illness, he's the one who'll be able to tell me. But every time I almost mention it, it sounds too weird to say. *So, uh, Mr. Polselli, when other people see the "turn off your cell phones" screen in the movie theater, I see an extra five-second movie trailer. Er . . . and did I mention I see stills of it on the billboard by my house? You see Jose Cuervo, I see a truck hitting a building and everything exploding. Is that normal?*

The first time was in the theater on the one holiday that our parents don't make us work—Christmas Day. I poked my younger sister, Rowan. "Did you see that?"

She did this eyebrow thing that basically says she thinks I'm an idiot. "See what?"

"The explosion," I said softly.

"You're on drugs." Rowan turned to our older brother, Trey, and said, "Jules is on drugs."

Trey leaned over Rowan to look at me. "Don't do drugs," he said seriously. "Our family has enough problems."

I rolled my eyes and sat back in my seat as the real movie trailers started. "No kidding," I muttered. And I reasoned with myself. The day before I'd almost been robbed while doing a pizza delivery. Maybe I was still traumatized.

I just wanted to forget about it all.

But then on MLK Day this stupid vision thing decided to get personal.

Two

Five reasons why I, Jules Demarco, am shunned:

1. I smell like pizza
2. My parents make us drive a meatball-topped food truck to school for advertising
3. I haven't invited a friend over since second grade
4. Did I mention I smell like pizza? Like, its umami[1]-ness oozes from my pores
5. Everybody at school likes Sawyer Angotti's family's restaurant better

Frankly, I don't blame them. I'd shun me too.

---

[*]look it up

Every January my mother says Martin Luther King Jr. weekend gives us the boost we need to pay the rent after the first two dead weeks of the year. She's superpositive about everything. It's like she forgets that every month is the same. Her attitude is probably what keeps our business alive. But if my mother, Paula, is the backbone of Demarco's Pizzeria, my father, Antonio, is the broken leg that keeps us struggling to catch up.

There's no school on MLK Day, so Trey and I are manning the meatball truck in downtown Chicago, and Rowan is working front of house in the restaurant for the lunch shift. She's jealous. But Trey and I are the oldest, so we get to decide.

The food truck is actually kind of a blast, even if it does have two giant balls on top, with endless jokes to be made. Trey and I have been cooking together since we were little—he's only sixteen months older than me. He's a senior. He's supposed to be the one driving the food truck to school because he has his truck license now, but he pays me ten bucks a week to secretly drive it so he can bum a ride from our neighbor Carter. Carter is kind of a douche, but at least his piece-of-crap Buick doesn't have a sack on its roof.

Trey drives now and we pass the billboard again.

"Hey—what was on the billboard?" I ask as nonchalantly as I can.

Trey narrows his eyes and glances at me. "Same as always. Jose Cuervo. Why?"

"Oh." I shrug like it's no big deal. "Out of the corner of my eye I thought it had changed to something new for once." Weak answer, but he accepts it. To me, the billboard is a still picture of the explosion. I look away and rub my temples as if it will make me see what everybody else sees, but it does nothing. Instead, I try to forget by focusing on my phone. I start posting all over the Internet where Demarco's Food Truck is going to be today. I'm sure some of our regulars will show up. It's becoming a sport, like storm chasing. Only they're giant meatball chasing.

Some people need a life. Including me.

We roll past Angotti's Trattoria on the way into the city—that's Sawyer's family's restaurant. Sawyer is working today too. He's outside sweeping the snow from their sidewalk. I beg for the traffic light to stay green so we can breeze past unnoticed, but it turns yellow and Trey slows the vehicle. "You could've made it," I mutter.

Trey looks at me while we sit. "What's your rush?"

I glance out the window at Sawyer, who either hasn't noticed our obnoxious food truck or is choosing to ignore it.

Trey follows my glance. "Oh," he says. "The enemy. Let's wave!"

I shrink down and pull my hat halfway over my eyes.

"Just . . . hurry," I say, even though there's nothing Trey can do. Sawyer turns around to pick up a bag of rock salt for the ice, and I can tell he catches sight of our truck. His head turns slightly so he can spy on who's driving, and then he frowns.

Trey nods coolly at Sawyer when their eyes meet, and then he faces forward as the light finally changes to green. "Do you still like him?" he asks.

Here's me, sunk down in the seat like a total loser, trying to hide, breathing a sigh of relief when we start rolling again. "Yeah," I say, totally miserable. "Do you?"

Three

Trey smiles. "Nah. That urban underground thing he's got going on is nice, and of course I'm fond of the, ah, Mediterranean complexion, but I've been over him for a while. He's too young for me. You can have him."

I laugh. "Yeah, right. Dad will love that. Maybe me hooking up with an Angotti will be the thing that puts him over the edge." I don't mention that Sawyer won't even look at me these days, so the chance of me "having" Sawyer is zero.

Sawyer Angotti is not the kind of guy most people would say is hot, but Trey and I have the same taste in men, which is sometimes convenient and sometimes a pain in the ass. Sawyer has this street casual look where he could totally be a clothes model, but if he ever told people he was one, they'd be like, "Seriously? No way." Because his most attractive features are so subtle, you know? At first glance he's really ordinary, but if you study him . . . big sigh. His vulnerable smile is what gets me—not the charming one he uses on teachers and girls and probably customers, too. I mean the warm, crooked smile that doesn't come out unless he's feeling shy or self-conscious. That one makes my stomach flip. Because for the most part, he's tough-guy metro, if such a thing exists. Arms crossed and eyebrow raised, constantly questioning the world. But I've seen his other side a million times. I've been in love with him since we played plastic cheetahs and bears together at indoor recess in first grade.

How was I supposed to know back then that Sawyer was the enemy? I didn't even know his last name. And I didn't know about the family rivalry. But the way my father interrogated me after they went to my first parent-teacher conference and found out that I "played well with others" and "had a nice friend in Sawyer Angotti," you'd have thought I'd given away great-grandfather's last weapon to the enemy. Trey says that was right around the time Dad really started acting weird.

All I knew was that I wasn't allowed to play cheetahs and bears with Sawyer anymore. I wasn't even supposed to talk to him.

But I still did, and he still did, and we would meet

under the slide and trade suckers from the candy jar each of our restaurants had by the cash register. I would bring him grape, and he always brought me butterscotch, which we never had in our restaurant. I'd do anything to get Sawyer Angotti to give me a butterscotch sucker again.

I have a notebook from sixth grade that has nine pages filled with embarrassing and overdramatic phrases like "I pine for Sawyer Angotti" and "JuleSawyer forever." I even made an *S* logo for our conjoined names in that one. Too bad it looks more like a cross between a dollar sign and an ampersand. I'd dream about us getting secretly married and never telling our parents.

And back then I'd moon around in my room after Rowan was asleep, pretending my pillow was Sawyer. Me and my Sawyer pillow would lie down on my bed, facing one another, and I'd imagine us in Bulger Park on a blanket, ignoring the tree frogs and pigeons and little crying kids. I'd touch his cheek and push his hair back, and he'd look at me with his gorgeous green eyes and that crooked, shy grin of his, and then he'd lean toward me and we'd both hold our breath without realizing it, and his lips would touch mine, and then . . . He'd be my first kiss, which I'd never forget. And no matter how much our parents tried to keep us apart, he'd never break my heart.

Oh, sigh.

But then, on the day before seventh grade started,

when it was time to visit school to check out classes and get our books, his father was there with him, and my father was there with me, and I did something terrible.

Without thinking, I smiled and waved at my friend, and he smiled back, and I bit my lip because of love and delight after not seeing him for the whole summer . . . and his father saw me. He frowned, looked up at my father, scowled, and then grabbed Sawyer's arm and pulled him away, giving my father one last heated glance. My father grumbled all the way home, issuing half-sentence threats under his breath.

And that was the end of that.

I don't know what his father said or did to him that day, but by the next day, Sawyer Angotti was no longer my friend. Whoever said seventh grade is the worst year of your life was right. Sawyer turned our friendship off like a faucet, but I can't help it—my faucet of love has a really bad leak.

Trey parks the truck as close to the Field Museum as our permit allows, figuring since the weather is actually sunny and not too freezing and windy, people might prefer to grab a quick meal from a food truck instead of eating the overpriced generic stuff inside the tourist trap.

Before we open the window for business, we set up. Trey checks the meat sauce while I grate fresh mozzarella into tiny, easily meltable nubs. It's a simple operation—our winter truck specialty is an Italian bread bowl with spicy mini meatballs, sauce, and cheese. The truth is it's delicious, even though I'm sick to death of them.

We also serve our pizza by the slice, and we're talking deep-dish Chicago-style, not that thin crap that Angotti's serves. Authentic, authschmentic. The tourists want the hearty, crusty, saucy stuff with slices of sausage the diameter of my bicep and bubbling cheese that stretches the length of your forearm. That's what we've got, and it's amazing.

Oh, but the Angotti's sauce . . . I had it once, even though in our house it's contraband. Their sauce will lay you flat, seriously. It's that good. We even have the recipe, apparently, but we can't use it because it's patented and they sell it by the jar—it's in all the local stores and some regional ones now too. My dad about had an aneurysm when that happened. Because, according to Dad, in one of his mumble-grumble fits, the Angottis had been after our recipe for generations and somehow managed to steal it from us.

So I guess that's how the whole rivalry started. From what I understand, and from what I know about Sawyer avoiding me like the plague, his parents feel the same way about us as my parents feel about them.

Trey and I pull off a really decent day of sales for the middle of January. We hightail it back home for the dinner rush so we can help Rowan out.

As we get close, we pass the billboard from the other side. I locate it in my side mirror, and it's the same as this morning. Explosion. I watch it grow small and disappear, and then close my eyes, wondering what the hell is wrong with me.

We pull into the alley and park the truck, take the stuff inside.

"Get your asses out there!" Rowan hisses as she flies through the kitchen. She gets a little anxious when people have to wait ten seconds. That kid is extremely well put together, but she carries the responsibility of practically the whole country on her shoulders.

Mom is rolling out dough. I give her a kiss on the cheek and shake the bank bag in her face to show her I'm on the way to putting it in the safe like I'm supposed to. "Pretty good day. Had a busload of twenty-four," I say.

"Fabulous!" Mom says, way too perky. She grabs a tasting utensil, reaches into a nearby pot, and forks a meatball for me. I let her shove it into my mouth when I pass her again.

"I's goo'!" I say. And really freaking hot. It burns the roof of my mouth before I can shift it between my teeth to let it cool.

Tony, the cook who has been working for our family restaurant for something like forty million years, smiles at me. “Nice work today, Julia,” he says. Tony is one of the few people I allow to call me by my birth name.

I guess my dad, Antonio, was actually named after Tony. Tony and my grandfather came to America together. I don’t really remember my grandpa much—he killed himself when I was little. Depression. A couple of years ago I accidentally found out it was suicide when I overheard Mom and Aunt Mary talking about it.

When I asked my mom about it later, she didn’t deny it—instead, she said, “But you kids don’t have any sign of depression in you, so don’t worry. You’re all fine.” Which was about the best way to make me think I’m doomed.

It’s a weird thing to find out about your family, you know? It made me feel really different for the rest of the day, and it still does now whenever I think about it. Like we’re all wondering where the depression poison will hit next, and we’re all looking at my dad. I wonder if that’s why my mother is so upbeat all the time. Maybe she thinks she can protect us with her happy shield.

Trey and I hurry to wash up, grab fresh aprons, and check in with Aunt Mary at the hostess stand. She’s seating somebody, so we take a look at the chart and see that the house is pretty full. No wonder Rowan’s freaking out.

Rowan’s fifteen and a freshman. Just as Trey is sixteen months older than me, she’s sixteen months younger. I don’t know if my parents planned it, and I don’t want to know, but there it is. I pretty much think they had us for the sole purpose of working for the family business. We started washing dishes and busing tables years ago. I'm not sure if it was legal, but it was definitely tradition.

Rowan looks relieved to see us. She's got the place under control, as usual. "Hey, baby! Go take a break," I whisper to her in passing.

"Nah, I'm good. I'll finish out my tables," she says. I glance at the clock. Technically, Rowan is supposed to quit at seven, because she's not sixteen yet—she can only work late in the summer—but, well, tradition trumps rules sometimes. Not that my parents are slave drivers or anything. They're not. This is just their life, and it's all they know.

It's a busy night because of the holiday. Busy is good. Busy means we can pay the rent, and whatever else comes up. Something always does.

By ten thirty all the customers have left. Even though Dad hasn't come down at all this evening to help out, Mom says she and Tony can handle closing up alone, and she sends Trey and me upstairs to the apartment to get some sleep.

I don't want to go up there.

Neither does Trey.

Four

Trey and I go out the back and into the door to the stairs leading up to our home above the restaurant. We pick our way up the stairs, through the narrow aisle that isn't piled with stuff. At the top, we push against the door and squeeze through the space.

Rowan has already done what she could with the kitchen. The sink is empty, the counters are clean. The kitchen is the one sacred spot, the one room where Mom won't take any garbage from anybody—literally. Because even after cooking all day, she still likes to be able to cook at home too, without having to worry that Dad's precious stacks of papers are going to combust and set the whole building on fire because they're too close to the gas stove.

Everywhere else—dining room, living room, and

hallway—is piled high around the edges with Dad's stuff. Lots of papers—recipes and hundreds of cooking magazines, mostly, and all the Chicago newspapers from the past decade. Shoe boxes, shirt boxes, and every other possible kind of box you can imagine, some filled with papers, some empty. Plastic milk crates filled with cookbooks and science books and gastronomy magazines. Bags full of greeting cards, birthday cards, sympathy cards, some written in, some brand-new, meant for good intentions that never happened. Hundreds of old videos, and a stack as high as my collarbone of old VCRs that don't work. Stereos, 8-track players, record players, tape recorders, all broken. Records and cassette tapes and CDs and games—oh my dog, the board games. Monopoly, Life, Password, Catch Phrase. Sometimes five or six duplicates, most of them with little yellowing masking-tape stickers on them that say seventy-five cents or a buck twenty-five. Insanity. Especially when somebody puts something heavy on top of a Catch Phrase and that stupid beeper goes off somewhere far below, all muffled.

We weave through it. Thankfully, Dad is nowhere to be found, either asleep or buried alive under all his crap. It's not like he's violent or mean or anything. He's just . . . unpredictable. When he's feeling good, he's in the restaurant. He's visible. He's easy to keep track of. But on the days he doesn't come down, we never know what to expect.

We climb those stairs after the end of our shift knowing he could be standing right there in the kitchen, long-faced, unshaven, having surfaced to eat something for the first time since yesterday. And rattling off the same guilt-inspired apologies, day after day after day. *I just couldn't make it down today. Not feeling up to it. I'm sorry you kids have to work so hard.* What do you say to that after the tenth time, or the hundredth?

Worse, he could be sitting in the dark living room with his hands covering his face, the blue glow from the muted TV spotlighting his depressed existence so we can't ignore it. It's probably wrong that Trey and Rowan and I all hope he stays invisible, holed up in his bedroom on days like these, but it's just easier when he's out of sight. We can pretend depressed Dad doesn't exist.

Tonight we breathe a sigh of relief. Trey heads into the cluttered bathroom, its cupboards overflowing with enough soap, shampoo, toothpaste, and toilet paper to get us through Y3K. Thank God our bedrooms are off-limits to Dad. I peek into my tidy little room and see Rowan is sleeping in her bed already, but I'm still wired from a long day. I close the door quietly and grab a glass of milk from the kitchen, then settle down in the one chair in the living room that's not full of stuff and flip on the TV. I run through the DVR list, choosing a rerun of an old Sherlock Holmes movie that I've been watching a little bit at a time over the past couple of weeks, whenever I get a chance. Somebody else must be watching it too, because it's not cued up to the last part I watched. I hit the slowest fast-forward so I can find where I left off.

Trey peeks his head in the room. "Night," he says. He dangles the keys to the meatball truck, and when I hold out my hand, he tosses them to me.

"Thanks," I say, not meaning it. I shouldn't have agreed to only ten bucks a week, but I was desperate. It's not nearly enough to pay for the humiliation of driving the giant balls. "Where's my ten bucks?"

"Isn't it only eight if one day is a holiday?" He gives me what he thinks is his adorable face and hands me a five and three ones.

"Sorry. Not in the contract." I hold my hand out for more.

"Dammit." He goes back to his room for two more dollars while Sir Henry on the TV is flitting around outside on the moors in fast mode, which looks kind of kooky.

Trey returns. "Here."

I grab the two bucks from him and shove all ten into my pocket with my tips. "Thanks. Night."

When he's gone, I stop the fast-forward, knowing I went too far, and rewind to the commercial as I slip the keys into my other pocket, then press play.

Instead of the movie that I'm expecting, I see *it* again.

It flashes by in a few seconds, and then it's gone. The truck, the building, the explosion. And then back to our regularly scheduled programming.

"Stop it," I whisper. My stomach flips and a creepy shiver runs down my neck. It makes my throat tighten. I pause the recording and sit there a minute, trying to calm down. And then I hit rewind.

Ninety-nine percent of me hopes there's nothing there but a creepy giant hound on the moor.

But there it is.

I watch it again, and I get this gnawing thing in my chest, like I'm supposed to do something about it.

"Why does this keep happening?" I mutter, and rewind it again. I hit play and it all flies by so fast, I can hardly see it. I rewind once more and this time set it to play in slow motion.

The truck is yellow. I notice it's actually a snowplow, and the snow is falling pretty hard. It's dark outside, but the streetlamps are lit. The truck is coming fast and it starts angling slightly, crossing to the wrong side and going off the road. It jumps the curb spastically and jounces over some snow piles in a big parking lot, and then I see the building—there's a large window—for a split second before the truck hits it. The building explodes shortly after contact, glass and brick shrapnel flying everywhere. The scene cuts to the body bags in the snow. I count again to make sure—definitely nine. The last frame is a close-up of three of the bags, and then it's over. I hit the pause button.

"What are you doing?"

I jump and whirl around to see Rowan standing in the doorway squinting at me, hair all disheveled. "Jeez!" I whisper, trying to calm my heartbeat. "You scared the crap out of me." I glance back at the TV with slow-motion dread, like I've just been caught looking at . . . I don't know. Porn, or something else I'm not supposed to look at. But it's paused at a sour cream commercial. I let out a breath of relief and turn my attention back to Rowan.

She shrugs. "Sorry. I thought I heard Mom come up."

"Not yet. Not for a while."

She scratches her head, the sleeve of her boy jammies wagging against her cheek. "You coming to bed soon? Or do you want me to stay up with you?"

Her sweet, sleepy disposition is one of my favorites, maybe because she can be so mellow and generous when she just wakes up. I suck in my bottom lip, thinking, and look at the remote control in my hand. "Nah, I'm coming to bed now. Just gotta brush my teeth."

She scrunches up her face and yawns. "What time is it?"

I laugh softly. "Around eleven, I guess. Eleven fifteen."

"Okay," she says, turning to go back down the hallway to our bedroom. "Night."

I look at the TV once more and close my weary eyes for a moment. Then I turn it off and stand up, setting the remote on top of the set so it doesn't get buried, and carefully pick my way to the bathroom, and on to bed. But I don't think I'll be sleeping anytime soon.

LISA McMANN

is the author of the *New York Times* bestselling Wake trilogy, *Cryer's Cross*, *Dead to You*, and the middle-grade dystopian fantasy series The Unwanteds. She lives with her family in the Phoenix area. Read more about Lisa and find her blog through her website at LISAMcMANN.COM or, better yet, find her on Facebook (facebook.com/mcmannfan) or follow her on Twitter (twitter.com/lisa_mcmann).